CW00493471

The
FlipFlopPsycho
&
The Philosophers Hat

ENJOY YOUR HOLIDAY

Ash Lawrence

PLEASE CONNECT WITH ME ON SOCIAL MEDIA!..

The FlipFlopPsycho and The Philosophers Hat.

DEDICATION

To my lovely wife Sarah for her never ending faith in my very bi-polar behaviour. Always keeping me focused on the important things in life and business. Even the best coaches in the world need a great coach. Sarah, my wife, my partner, my rock!

FOREWORD

Have you ever worked with a mentor or coach that you've been working with where you're keeping a tally at the top of your notes tracking and you realise you're giving them more in the session than you're getting back!

Yes.. that's definitely been me many times!

Until... I met Ash Lawrence.

I've known Ash for over 10 years. Having met him at an ABC networking event he has become a great mentor and friend. Ash is like Marmite. You either love him, or you dislike him! Why would you dislike him? Well... he will tell you what he thinks and what he sees. For some, they don't like hearing the truth.

Over the years I've attended many of Ash's programmes, Millionaire Mindset, Entrepreneurs Business Club and the MAD group, and I've had regular one to one coaching sessions for mindset development. Ash is someone I respect, trust and I love his down to earth advice that kicks me straight back onto my journey of vision.

Myself, I've been in business over 11 and a half years. I run a successful social media agency, have spoken in over 14 countries across the world and regularly appear on TV - BBC World News, BBC, and had the honour of sitting on the famous sofa with Eamon and Ruth. I've worked with some amazing brands including; NATO, Ann Summers, Mercure hotels and many more. I also work with many small businesses guiding them on their social media journeys.

Working with Ash has definitely brought me further on my journey and made me look at different situations in alternative ways.

I am a sucker for reading books and love getting to know well-known business leaders, their journeys and the strategies they have taken to grow their businesses.

Have you ever read a business book that's full of statistics, examples you can't relate to and has inspirational quotes that you can't fathom? Yes... that's me!

Until I read **The FlipFlopPsycho & The Philosophers Hat**

A book full of wisdom, relatable examples and tactics you can take away and start to action. I, for one have started to action using many of the tactics inside this book, and can definitely relate to some of the stories that Ash shares.

Just starting with the first chapter... this was definitely me! Worrying about what other people think and allowing it to hold me back from living my dreams, going forward with a goal. Halting me when I came to an obstacle and not want to step forward as I was worried about what people thought.

I used to question myself "Why?", "Why, do I worry?". Having had the pleasure of reading The FlipFlopPsycho and the Philosophers Hat before it's formal publication has enabled me to "let go" of a few beliefs I've been holding onto and understanding why I did.

If you're a business owner, entrepreneur or someone looking to understand why we think the way we do, I would urge you to jump straight in, take some time out, grab your favourite drink and read this book. It will allow you to see things in a different way, but only if you allow it!

I urge you to be true to yourself, read this book with an open mind, no expectations or limitations. Answer this question "Is this me?" at the end of each story, tell yourself "I am going to action these steps" to make a difference.

Don't just read it once. Treat this as a book that's handy when you have a blip, negative day, or feel you want to react. A book you can pick up at any time to guide you through a situation. An honest book that speaks the truth.

So... what are you waiting for... To Your Successes...
Zoe

Ash Lawrence

INTRODUCTION

When I was a boy my dad would keep coming up with these quotes and I used to think *'What a load of old rubbish!'* and *'What has that got to do with reality?'*

As I've got older I've realised that these 2000 year old quotes are still very pertinent today, it's just that because they've been around forever we naturally think here comes another cliché and we don't really put any real value or meaning to them.

So I thought it would be good to look at these ancient stoic sayings and see what they could and do mean today.

There are 25 quotes and then the modern day interpretation with some action points.

Like anything in life, you must take action on what you learn otherwise you may as well not learnt it.

Information without implementation equals stagnation.

ACKNOWLEDGMENTS

A massive thank you to **Claire Osborne** who's copywriting and research skills are absolutely outstanding and without whom this book would never have been published!

Carrie Stay for another creative book cover design.

Zoe Cairns for her consistent, positive support and the Foreword.

Rachel Cowell for getting me out of trouble with the spelling! She's not only a great editor, she owns a very successful clothing, merchandising and branding business. JustSo Ltd!

Sally Brady The #CashFlowLady for the review.

The FlipFlopPsycho and The Philosophers Hat.

CONTENTS

Foreword v

Introduction vii

Acknowledgements vii

1 Amaze me 3

2 No great thing 8

3 Quality of a fool 14

4 No person has the power 20

5 Change a situation 25

6 People are frugal 29

7 Upset you 35

8 Conquer the world 40

9 Study the past 47

10	Follow the herd	53
11	Action steps	57
12	Foolish one	64
13	What you would be	69
14	Don't explain	74
15	External things	80
16	Begin to speak	85
17	How long	90
18	Waste time	96
19	Often frightened	101
20	Which port	106
21	Living now	111
22	Like a puppet	116
23	Stupid by necessity	122
24	Like a river	127
25	Does not learn	132

The FlipFlopPsycho and The Philosophers Hat.

1. AMAZE ME

'It never ceases to amaze me: we all love ourselves more than other people, but care more about their opinion than our own.' - Marcus Aurelius

Ok, so you might have instantly taken offence to the first part of this quote.

I can hear you now...

"*I absolutely do NOT love myself more than I love anyone else! I always put others first!!*", and while I'm not saying this isn't true, it's not really what Marcus Aurelius was saying. It's less about ego (which is a thing that exists for all of us, obviously), and more about human nature.

Every living organism's top priority is its own survival. Even the most selfless person in the world is hardwired to look out for number one first in order to stay alive – the survival instinct is STRONG. And I think that's what our mate Marcus was going for here: Even though our own well-being and personal preference are so important to us, when it comes to matters of opinion, we will normally look to others and be swayed by what they think or say - even if our own opinion is different.

You know how it goes; someone tells you your crap at something enough times and eventually you start to believe it!

Have your mates spent years ribbing you about how bad you are chatting to members of the opposite sex - all because you crashed and burned one time in a nightclub about a million years ago? Chances are you now consider yourself a bit of a loser in love and don't bother putting yourself out there anymore.

Ever asked a friend for an opinion on your outfit and ended up getting changed before you went out because they were less than complimentary?

I bet you never wore it again - or certainly saw it in a different light. I mean, those are pretty cliche examples, but the fact is, even if you LOVE that dress, or thought that you communicated and engaged well with others in social situations - it seems to be that, for a lot of us, it's what other people think that counts. Whether that opinion is solicited or not.

Of course, the effect of other people's opinions works the other way too.

It could be that because of positive opinions that other people have given you that you feel smarter, more attractive or more talented than you previously thought you were. Either way, the point is that whatever it is that we think of ourselves, we're still more likely to listen to other people, and believe them.

There is a chance that this could lead to a great ego boost of course, and to feeling good about ourselves. Listening to great opinions of ourselves from others can make us more motivated, more determined - in fact, when the opinions of our peers are favourable, the high it gives us can become addictive. But, more often than not, it is the 'bad' opinions that we're more likely to listen to, remember, and take to heart - and that can be a killer for your self-esteem.

The question is, why *do* we ask for or listen to other people's opinions in the first place?.....and more importantly - why do we give a shit?

As I said earlier, it's hardwired in humans to survive - and that includes surviving as part of a social group.

It's evolution - safety in numbers, and all that; protection from predators, working together in order to have enough to eat etc. In this modern age the desire to fit in with our peers is still a part of our DNA, but whereas our ancestors didn't want to be cast out from the group for being weak or injured, we don't want to be outcasts for wearing the 'wrong' trainers or acting the 'wrong' way.

We all want to be liked and accepted - but it comes at a cost.

Seeking approval from others is so deeply ingrained that, for a lot of people, worrying about other people's opinions can cause mental health issues such as anxiety or depression. It can affect our confidence, the way we go about things, and stop us from enjoying what we love or being who we really are for fear of other people thinking badly of us.

It's a sad fact that what others think of us becomes more important than what we think about ourselves. Desperately seeking 'good' opinions from other people can leave us exhausted; trying to prove that we are hard-working enough, cool enough, successful enough...it's as if our self-worth and value is hinging on everyone else.

Of course, I'm sure you know someone who genuinely doesn't give a flying fuck what anyone thinks about them and what they do or how they live - and I bet they're always really happy.

So, why is it that some of us are more vulnerable to caring about opinions outside of our own than others?

Nine times out of ten it's something echoing from our past. Someone present in our younger years might have made us feel that affection and praise was conditional - something we didn't necessarily deserve. If that's the case, you might experience feelings of shame if something you do isn't 'perfect'.

Maybe the people who cared for you during your childhood were abusive, emotionally distant, or set impossible standards. Or perhaps you've been bullied - either at school or as an adult.

It could be none of those things. Something you can't pinpoint or explain. All you know is that you don't feel like you measure up, you feel unworthy and insecure, and so you seek the reassurances of others in order to feel like you matter.

You might have already realised that It's somewhat ironic. That needing other people's opinions to make you happy, is what's making you unhappy.

So, how can you stop needing this?

How can you create a new mindset?

It's All About Perspective

This sounds a bit harsh, but you really wouldn't care about the opinions of other people if you really knew how little people think about you.

And I really don't mean that in the 'no one cares about/likes you' sense.

What I mean is, everyone's got their own shit going on. All they're really invested in is their own success, careers, families, relationships. This doesn't mean that they're not kind, caring people - it's just that for the most part, people only really care about what directly affects them.

Stop Trying To Be Perfect

Let's face it - perfection doesn't exist, it's an illusion, and you need to stop feeling that if you can do something 'right', then people will only think good things about you. It sounds cliche, but it's true: what someone else thinks about you says more about them than it does about you.

Get To Know You

Are you really living your best life, or are the choices you make about your career, your relationships etc just to please someone else?

Do you really enjoy the things you do, the way you act, the way you dress...or are you trying to impress someone else?

Get to know yourself - let yourself try new things....ask yourself, 'what might I enjoy or pursue if I wasn't so worried about other people's opinions?'

Probably a lot.

Be Vulnerable

No one wants to be the person who takes a risk, speaks out, and goes against the grain - not least of all because we tend to fear disapproval. But honestly, sometimes, you just have to go for it.

You can't grow as a person if you always play it safe because you're too afraid to fail. Remember that.

Like Yourself

It's a hard fact that you'll never please everyone - no matter what you do. There will always be someone who has an opinion of you or what you do that will make you feel like shit.

But that goes for everyone. Which is quite a comforting thought.

All you can do is please yourself - like YOU, and the things that YOU do, and the decisions that YOU make. It's OK to ask people's opinions, and a lot of them will think you're awesome. Others won't - and that's OK TOO.

Do it anyway.

2. NO GREAT THING

"No great thing is created suddenly, any more than a bunch of grapes or a fig. If you tell me that you desire a fig, I answer that there must be time. Let it first blossom, then bear fruit, then ripen." — Epictetus

This is quite a flowery quote from Epictetus, but we all know some other version of this don't we?

Patience is a virtue. Good things come to those who wait. Shit doesn't just *happen*.

Basically, we have to put time and effort into the things that we want to be successful in. We have to plant the seeds and nurture the plant, tend to it carefully and help it to grow in order to enjoy the delicious fruit. In the fast-paced world that we live in today, that can be quite difficult - especially in this age of instant gratification where we want everything yesterday.

We know that it's important to be patient, we're told that enough as kids, but it's not something that is innate within us - we have to consciously learn - but it's not something a lot of us are ever really taught. Like most things, patience is a discipline and something that we need to practice.

Of course Epictetus's quote can be applied to everything we want to be successful at in life - and not least our business goals. It takes time and patience to come up with a business plan, to build employee and client relations, to negotiate, to communicate, and to ultimately become successful.

It might seem that rushing full-steam ahead is going to be more fruitful (we all want to beat the competition and get in there first, don't we!?), but the truth is that being patient and taking your time to achieve your goals is the only way to really learn to adapt to unforeseen changes and overcome any obstacles that stand in our way on the path to success.

If you're still of the mindset that slow and steady *doesn't* win the race, and that you don't have time to waste by waiting, let me spell out the benefits of practicing patience for you...

Patience Prevents Frustration

If you're someone who finds nothing more frustrating than having to wait for more than five minutes for *anything*, you might find this one hard to believe - but keep reading.

Impatient people are simply unable to delay gratification, and it's THAT which causes the frustration. The knock-on effect of this is that frustration is the emotional energy that causes us to quit things, which is why when you're not reaching your goals fast enough, you end up chucking the towel in and starting all over again. For impatient people, this is a pattern that is doomed to be repeated.

Patience Leads To Smarter Decisions

If you want to make good decisions for your business, your health, your finances, your relationships.....then patience is one of your key resources.

Patience really is a virtue; one that keeps us from second-guessing ourselves or listening to negative sources that might cloud our judgement. It also makes us much more likely to stop and focus on the present moment - and when we do that, we are able to take the small AND big picture into account before we make decisions and choices.

That's not to say that practicing patience will make you infallible - you're still human after all, but by learning to take your time, being mindful, and not rushing things, the decisions you make are sure to be wiser ones.

Patience Can Build Your Reputation

Let's say you want to get a cake made for your kid's birthday, and there are two bakers you know of in town.

Do you go with the one who could do it at really short notice, but who has a reputation for cutting corners and sometimes being a bit shoddy, or the one who's going to take a lot longer, but has never had an unsatisfied customer?

It's obvious isn't it. Patience helps us to work steadily towards our goals, and if we reach those goals over and over again, the word's going to get out - which is great for business. A good reputation comes from perseverance - not from saying, 'that'll do, the icing's not really set properly, and those marzipan decorations are definitely going to fall off before they get it home - but it's done' (or words to that effect anyway).

Basically, success comes from dedicating ourselves and putting in effort, not looking for shortcuts or giving up. That's not to say that practicing patience always means that the cake is going to take us ages, just that we have to be patient with our progress, whether it's fast or slow.

Ok, enough with the cakes, you get the idea.

Patience Makes Us Feel In Control

When we actually take the time to let something grow, we're also giving ourselves the time to choose how to act and respond to events and situations, rather than making knee jerk decisions or allowing our emotions to take over.

No matter what is happening around you, if you can stay in control, you can handle anything.

It's the feeling of not being in control that is most people's reason for being impatient - and then we're back to frustration again! Not being patient affects our judgement and our ability to plan things, communicate with others, and gives us unrealistic expectations about what we can achieve - and when.

Patience Makes Us More Tolerant

Impatience and intolerance go hand in hand.

Patience helps us to expect obstacles in life and gives us the tools to deal with them - such as optimism and courage, meaning we're more likely to roll up our sleeves and 'get on with it', rather than starting to feel overwhelmed and bitter when it feels like everything's going wrong.

Rolling with the punches means we experience less stress and builds our resilience - fantastic traits if you're trying to build a business or lead a team.

Patience Gives Us Hope

When we're rushing through life and getting impatient that things aren't going our way right NOW, it can be impossible to see a good outcome. A patient person doesn't give up, they keep trying because they believe that their goals are possible, and they understand that just because success is delayed doesn't mean it's not coming!

Patience Leads To Excellence

Excellence and success always begins with patience and commitment - you can't expect to achieve what you want overnight without putting in the time and effort. Being patient means that you'll make decisions based on facts, rather than acting impulsively, and ultimately setting yourself up for a fall.

Patience isn't easy to come by, you have to consciously practice it as part of your growth mindset. You have to learn that things worth having don't come easily, and it's patience that will stop you from quitting at the first hurdle.

It was Thomas Edison who said that, "Many of life's failures are people who did not realise how close they were to success when they gave up" and there's so much truth at the heart of that.

Being impatient means that you won't notice the doors of opportunity opening for you. You're just going to throw your hands up the second something goes wrong and abandon your goals.

Patience is the greatest tool in your tool box when it comes to any goal you want to achieve. Want to lose weight, hit the gym and transform your body? You're not going to drop 10 pounds and get a six pack overnight - it takes patience, and those who aren't willing to be patient will soon get frustrated and quit.

If you're starting a new business, you're not going to build a reputation, a client list and huge profits overnight; it takes time and patience. You won't find your ideal partner by rushing into a serious relationship with the first person who comes along. You need to be patient getting to know people.

You won't find your dream home without patience. Without patience, you'll make quick, emotion-led decisions and possibly end up regretting one of the biggest purchases you'll ever make..... I could go on and on.

Whatever it is you want to achieve in life, practice patience, and you will be rewarded for it.

3. QUALITY OF A FOOL

It is the peculiar quality of a fool to perceive the faults of others and to forget his own." – Marcus Tullius Cicero

Have you ever noticed how everyone on the road is an absolute idiot - except you? Or how it's always someone else letting the side down at work? Perhaps you're the only one in the house who doesn't make a mess, or the only one in your friendship group who doesn't talk utter bollocks?

Same here. And everyone else for that matter; friends, family, work colleagues...they will all undoubtedly say the same if you ask them.

So, if you and everyone you know is, like Mary Poppins, practically perfect in every way - who are the morons?

"I'm alright, it's everyone else that's the problem" is an often-spoken phrase. But common sense has to tell us that it can't *always* be someone else that is at fault. Could it, sometimes, be *us?*

What is it that makes it so easy to spot faults and mistakes in others and their actions, but not our own? Are we all really 'fools', as Cicero said?

First of all, it's not just that you're a pompous arse. The tendency that we, as humans, have to spot other people's flaws and the cons before the pros, is known as The Negativity Instinct.

And that's *really* not our fault.

This instinct stems from evolution and is designed to increase our chances of survival, which makes sense when you think about it. Fear is a very powerful instinct that helps us stay alive. It's the reason we don't walk along the edge of cliffs, approach wild animals or take risks when we're driving etc.

This ingrained fear of dying is what has helped mankind identify dangers and steer us as well clear as possible from diseases and calamities since the dawn of time. Even though a lot of the dangers our ancestors faced no longer exist, our brains are still operating with the same software.

It is our in-built instinct to spot problems that make our minds swing towards the negatives first.

In our modern world this instinct still presents itself in our daily lives. Sure, we're unlikely to be attacked by wild animals when we step outside the front door, but that primal fear now shows itself in other ways - the fear of losing our jobs, of having a car accident, of being embarrassed, of our relationships failing.....these are the modern-day fears that make us shift the blame to other people - those we know as well as total strangers - basically, onto anyone except us.

We live in a bit of a blame culture don't we? All those 'where there's blame there's a claim' companies that cold-call us the second we trip over a loose paving slab would go out of business pretty quickly if we didn't! But what is the true cost of living a life where everyone is at fault apart from ourselves?

In order to find out, we first need to take a look at the self-serving bias - where the majority of us will quite happily take the credit when things are going great, but lay the blame elsewhere when things go bad.

Blaming the circumstances surrounding something not going our way is one thing, but when we start to blame people - especially the ones who are close to us - we can really end up damaging our careers, families and relationships.

So, why do we do it in the first place?

It's Easier

Blame = less accountability = less work. When we don't take any responsibility for the things that go wrong it means we don't have to make any effort to fix it. It's someone else's fault - therefore it's all on them!

It Makes Us Feel More In Control

If something is your own fault, you have to admit that you were a little bit (or a lot!) out of control. You're going to have to answer some potentially awkward questions and listen to people telling you where you went wrong. Not pleasant.

Blaming someone else means that you have control of the story - things happened the way they did because of someone else, and so you don't have to handle the situation any further.

Your Ego Is Protected

No one likes to lose face, and blaming someone else puts you in a superior position: you are 'good', the other person is 'bad'. Blame is status-seeking behaviour and is a way to compare ourselves favourably to our peers.

Of course, there are people who use blame to make themselves look like a victim. Again, this is a form of social comparison; when we are in 'woe is me' mode, we are still the 'good' person, and get lots of positive attention to boot.

With me so far? Making everything someone else's fault is a self-preservation tactic that is an easy way out AND strokes our ego a bit. But, by only finding the fault in others and not in ourselves, what do we stand to lose.

As it turns out, quite a lot!

Personal Growth

What we're really doing when we are blind to our own faults and constantly blame others is displaying a defence mechanism, protecting ourselves against criticism and judgement.

Unfortunately, a by-product of this self-defence is that we deny ourselves the chance to learn and grow from what others have to teach us.

If we can't learn from our mistakes or recognise our own faults that have contributed to the situation, we're in for a lifetime of shirking the responsibility and shifting the blame to others - essentially leaving us stuck in a pattern of behaviour that is self-destructive.

Our Empathy

If you're someone who uses blame to avoid being held accountable for your actions, it stops you from listening to how others feel and accepting it, and eventually not being able to feel empathy.

It might sound dramatic - of course you empathise with how other people feel! But think about it: if your go-to trait when something goes tits up is to say that it's all someone else's fault, then that means in every situation that doesn't go the way you want, you're only thinking about how it affects you. Over time this will become a nasty habit.

In fact, research has shown that people who are self-obsessed (narcissists) are more prone to pass blame than anyone else. Pretty sure that's a label you don't want!

Our Relationships

If you're a blamer, it's highly unlikely that you have strong, healthy relationships with other people.

Why?

Well, let's imagine you have a tendency to blame your friend or partner for everything. It's their fault you were both late for that dinner reservation, their fault you slept in, that a bill didn't get paid on time...if you're refusing to admit that you too are bad at time-keeping, at money-management and at setting an alarm, or played any part at all in the situation, what you're essentially doing is keeping yourself 'good' and making them 'bad'.

This constant 'putting down' of your loved-one will eventually push them away. Reverse the situation for a second. If someone was constantly telling you that you were at fault, and they were completely blameless in every situation, would you want to be around them? Or would you constantly feel unworthy, judged and devalued?

Thought so.

Your Power

This is a big one, and is something you probably don't even think about when you're busy making everything everyone else's fault.

By blaming someone else you are making yourself completely powerless.

If it's not your fault then you have no power to change anything. The other person is completely in the driver's seat, and you are the helpless victim along for the ride. Doesn't feel good, does it?

So, now that I've proved how completely shitty it is for you, as well as other people, when you can't find fault with yourself, how can you stop yourself from doing it? After all, it is human nature; even young children will blame someone or something else for fear of getting into trouble when they mess up.

And, if you've realised after reading this that you're a serial blamer, and it's starting to affect your life in the ways that I've already mentioned, there are a couple of things you can do.

Build Your Self-Esteem

People who don't have a lot of self-worth are generally much quicker to blame someone else than take responsibility for themselves and their actions.

The more confident and self-assured you are as a person, the more likely you are to accept your own capacity for error AND the more likely you are to understand it in other people too - so it's a double whammy.

Positive, daily affirmations, such as telling yourself 'I am capable, I am enough' can boost your self-esteem over time, and eventually lead to you blaming other people for your failings less and less, and accepting that you are the one with the power to change things when they don't go your way.

Stop Telling The Tale

A story about blame, when told over and over again is like a snowball.

Bear with me.

It might start off small in your hands, but every time you tell someone this tale of how someone else is the reason stuff went wrong for you, that ball is picking up more and more snow as it rolls along, making you less and less responsible, and the other person even more so. Eventually you'll find you're just packing on snow in huge handfuls, blaming that poor sod for things that aren't even related to them!

In the end, it's all about perspective, and colouring our view of other people because we don't want to accept that we might have things about us that are 'bad' just leaves us with a bit of a foggy view.

So, the next time you're tempted to say that something is somebody else's fault, ask yourself if you played a part or maybe even the whole role in some cases! Take responsibility and in turn, your power back.

4. NO PERSON HAS THE POWER

"No person has the power to have everything they want, but it is in their power not to want what they don't have, and to cheerfully put to good use what they do have." – Seneca

It's a universal truth that we don't always get what we want in life. We can work hard, plan and be as optimistic as we like; but the fact is, things might not always work out for us. Most of us learnt that from a very young age - and it's not a bad lesson to learn to be honest. A more important lesson to learn is that we need to focus our energy on what we have, rather than what we don't.

That's right, folks - this one's about gratitude.

The benefits of gratitude have been well-studied. Feeling grateful is good for your psychological well-being, your relationships, and possibly even your physical health. But let's not pretend it's a feeling that comes easily to all of us.

Research has shown that the ability to feel grateful is deep-rooted in our brains, genes, and even our personalities. And if you're someone who finds it easier to lament what you don't have, rather than put to good use what you DO have, you'll be pleased to learn that gratitude isn't purely hard-wired. You can learn techniques that will bring more gratitude into your life.

Good news.

We're quite greedy by nature - we always want more: a bigger house, more money, a 'better' body....to be cleverer, more successful, more loved... and this want for 'more' makes it pretty easy to forget to STOP and show appreciation for the things we already have.

Let's face it - you might feel that you have less than some people, but you almost definitely have more than others.

So, there are techniques we can put into practice to help us show gratitude and therefore live happier lives - what are they?

Don't Be So Picky

There's no doubt in my mind that you'd feel a great deal of gratitude if you won the lottery this weekend, overcame a terrible illness, or were suddenly headhunted for a prestigious, well-paid position at your dream job. But your gratitude doesn't have to be reserved for the 'big' things.

Gratitude is a habit, and in order to get into that habit we need to recognise that nothing in our lives is too small to be grateful for. Great weather, getting straight through to someone on the phone rather than being on hold for ages, someone replying quickly to your important email, no queue at the petrol station...all things you can feel appreciation for.

And then there's the stuff in life that, while not necessarily 'small', we might take for granted: the roof over our head and the job that helps us to afford it, the food on our table, our family and friends, our health...

Sit and consciously think about all the things that you have to be grateful for and you'll find that the list is unending - even if those things aren't great riches, a mansion or a six pack.

Finding Gratitude In Difficult Situations

Alright, this one might sound a bit weird, but it's important to learn that gratitude isn't just about being thankful for the positives. Negative experiences, although unpleasant, can actually be really useful in helping to pinpoint the things we really have to be grateful for.

Admittedly it sometimes takes a little digging...

But let's say you've just been let go from your job. It sucks! Your overwhelming thoughts and feelings are going to be fear, anger, desperation...life is unfair...what will you do now? What on earth is there to be grateful for in this situation?

First of all, it's totally normal and OK to think and feel all of those things in the beginning - you'd be a bit weird if you didn't. But once you've calmed down, delve a little bit deeper and seize the positives.

Now you have no excuse not to pursue the career you've always wanted, or to start that new learning course, or take that trip you've always wanted to. Of course, these might not be things that you can do instantly - it might be a case of first, finding a job to keep the wolf from the door - AND, you now have an opportunity to think ahead and start planning for all the things you've been putting off because of the job you used to be in.

A relationship ending is another example. Once that first wave of emotions has worn off, you'll see that you are presented with opportunities you didn't have before. The chance to move to a different area of the country - or the world! To start that new hobby you've been putting off because you felt you didn't have the free time, and (harsh as it may sound), the chance to live your life exactly as you wish without having to consider how it will affect the other person.

Again, not things you might even think about to begin with when all you want to do is cry on the sofa with a bottle of vodka, much less feel grateful for, but the positives are there even in what is initially a negative situation.

Be Mindful

Knowing that you need to be grateful for the things you have - even when the chips are down - is one thing, but how can you actually practice it? This is where being mindful comes in.

Try and think of five to ten things to be grateful for every day (as I said earlier, they don't have to be huge, life-changing things) and actually sit and think about them.

Picture the things that you are thankful for in your mind and allow the feelings of gratitude to wash over you.

If you make it a habit to do this every day you can actually rewire your brain to start feeling grateful naturally and you'll feel happier every time you do it too.

It sounds like bullshit, but it seriously only takes about 8 weeks of literally practicing to be grateful for your brain patterns to change, allowing you to feel happier and more empathetic. Honestly, give it a go.

Keep A Gratitude Journal

You've been living under a rock if you haven't heard about gratitude journals or the benefits of keeping one, but just in case, allow me to enlighten you.

It's pretty much what it says on the tin: a journal in which you write down the things you are grateful for. After your mindfulness session, stick down all the things you're thankful for. It's a good way to consciously think about what you're grateful for without getting distracted by negative, ungrateful thoughts.

You can write in it every day after you've practiced gratitude, or you can come back to it each week or month. It's worth doing even if you don't feel like it's your 'thing'...it's a really good way to help you keep track of the positives in your life and it impacts on your brain to actually perform the action of writing.

Do Something For others

It sounds a bit cliche, but nothing reminds us more of what we have to be grateful for than to spend time with others who aren't as fortunate. So if you're someone who is really struggling to find something in your life that you can feel truly grateful for, and my tips aren't doing diddly squat - try this one:

Volunteer...

Giving back to others in your local community...

Volunteering at a homeless shelter, a children's hospital, a residential home etc - will certainly be a humbling experience, and one that will definitely make you more grateful for the things you've been taking for granted.

This isn't a way of punishing yourself, by the way; it's actually a pretty good gift to give yourself. By volunteering to help others, selflessly giving your time and energy, it actually increases your own well-being and your feelings of self-worth - with having more feelings of gratitude being a nice little bonus on the side.

So, there you have it. You might not always get everything you want, but there's always something in your life to be grateful for. So focus on that, and you'll find that once you start counting your blessings they'll multiply in abundance, and what you don't have won't seem important any more.

5. CHANGE A SITUATION

"When we are no longer able to change a situation, we are challenged to change ourselves." – Viktor Frankl

OK OK, I know, Victor Frankl didn't write this 2000 years ago! However, it is great wisdom and something I thought you would find of value!

At first glance this quote by Viktor Frankl is about giving up trying to change a bad situation, and in a way it is - there *are* certain situations we can't change. But, just because we can't change things externally, it doesn't mean we can't change things within ourselves instead. I'm talking mainly about changing our reaction and perception to things, along with our attitude (yes, I'm going to mention PMA today).

Changing these internal factors aren't always likely to change the situation, but it will change us, and this is what our mate, Viktor, is suggesting.

Let's face it, no one likes change - certainly not in all areas of life - but it's one of the only constant things in our lives, whether it be big changes, like people coming in and out of our lives, changes to our health or job, moving house, or everyday things like the changing of the seasons, that pub you love closing down, or your landlord putting the rent up.

We can't avoid change, and often the harder we try to resist, the more difficult we make things for ourselves. It can cause us stress and upset, confusion, anger...and just a general feeling that the rug has been whipped out from under our feet. Very unsettling.

Even those that we would consider 'good' changes; a new relationship or a promotion at work for example, can throw us into a bit of a tailspin and have a huge impact on our lives - IF we don't learn to adapt to that change.

And you might ask why do we have to?

Basically, if you're not prepared for change, and perhaps are even resistant to it, you'll end up feeling out of control of your own life and will end up limiting your own choices. A lot of unexpected changes (even those that we might call a 'crisis'), that happen in our lives can be great growing and learning opportunities.

By forcing us to step out of our comfort zone, these changes can offer us a challenge that, rising to, could lead to us becoming more resilient and stronger in character.

That all sounds great, obviously - who *doesn't* want to feel strong in the face of adversity, maturing and growing, seizing new opportunities as they present themselves?

Exactly. And if this positive mental attitude (PMA) (see, I told you I'd mention it) isn't something that comes easily to you, what strategies can you adopt that will help you adapt to change by changing yourself, when you can't change the situation itself?

Step 1: Change Your Mindset

George Bernard Shaw said that, *'Progress is impossible without change, and those who cannot change their minds cannot change anything'.*

Wise words. Basically he's talking about changing your mindset - and you know I LOVE to talk about the importance of the right mindset! Changing yours from a 'fixed' mindset; a place that makes you fear stepping out of your comfort zone and that is resistant to change, to a 'growth' mindset, that allows you to embrace change, is the best way to start adapting to situations that are out of your control. However, it might take a bit of practice!

Our subconscious doesn't like the 'unknown', and is why it is resistant to change, and why our self-limiting beliefs, fear and discomfort all rise to the surface when we're faced with an unfamiliar situation.

23

We have to *choose* to be positive about any changes that come our way.

The more we focus our minds on adapting to change the more resilient we become. After all, we can't control the events themselves, but we can decide how we react to them.

Step 2: Do Scary Things

I'm not suggesting swimming with sharks or skydiving necessarily, but doing things that take you out of your comfort zone is important for learning to adapt to change. Change is scary (maybe even scarier than sharks!), and by making our subconscious believe that doing scary things is a normal thing for us to do, it will become more familiar with the concept, and won't make you feel like running for the hills the next time a situation of change arises.

Make a list of stuff that you want to do but have always been too afraid to. Like I say, it doesn't have to be extreme; it could be eating a meal alone in a restaurant or joining an am dram group for example, but whatever it is, make a plan to do it and actually DO IT NOW!

The exhilaration of overcoming your fears is an amazing feeling, and over time those things that you used to view as 'scary' will no longer be so….eventually you'll be able to say the same about change!

Step 3: Have No Regrets

OK, I appreciate this one is easier said than done, and unless you can let things go, forgive and forget, and recognise when a situation is done, you really can't move forward.

Regrets have a huge impact on how you react to change, and can really hold you back. Think about it; changes present opportunities in your life, but if you're too busy looking back at the things you regret in the past, you're going to miss all the things that are open to you in the present and future.

Regret is such a futile emotion - you can't go backwards, you can't change what is already done - you have to choose to live in the present and move forwards into the future.

If you know that you are someone who has a tendency to live in the past, you're going to need to consciously change that, or else you're going to sabotage yourself at every turn.

Step 4: Find Your Purpose In Life

Alright, this one might take a while, especially if it's not something you've ever really thought about, but what is important in your life?

Knowing the answer will help you find purpose and sense of direction in your life, which will help massively when it comes to drive and focus - and having both of those will help you when it comes to adapting to life's changes.

Perhaps you have a deep held desire to help people, to create things, to raise a family, to educate yourself as much as you can, to see as much of the world as possible...

You don't have to have every second of your entire life mapped out in minute detail of course, but having no purpose or meaning at all normally means you're just drifting aimlessly around the comfort zone box you've built for yourself - and you won't find many opportunities in there!

Step 5: Live A Balanced And Healthy Life

Never underestimate how much living a healthy, active and balanced life can build our resilience and help us to manage the disruption that changes can have in our lives.

Stress can actually help us to perform BETTER in the short term, in fact, it's a normal response when it comes to dealing with the challenges we might face on a daily basis.

Constantly feeling stress can be problematic for our health. This is why it's important to find positive ways to deal with it, and healthy lifestyle changes such as exercising regularly, eating a healthy diet, getting enough sleep and reducing our alcohol and caffeine intake are all part of that.

It's not just about what we put into our bodies that we need to think of in order to lead a healthy balanced life. We need to consider our minds too, which is why taking a break from technology, spending time with people who make us feel good and learning meditation techniques are all important when it comes to coping with any changes that might come our way.

In life, we're all going to find ourselves in situations that we wish we could change. But more often than not we can't. All we can do is make ourselves as physically and mentally fit as possible to embrace anything that comes our way, by changing our attitude to the way we deal with things.

Nothing stays the same way forever, and we shouldn't either. By learning to adapt and 'roll with the punches' we can see the possibilities and opportunities in everything that comes our way, so, change that mindset, put on your grown-up pants, and start moving forward – embracing whatever change comes this way.

6. PEOPLE ARE FRUGAL

People are frugal in guarding their personal property; but as soon as it comes to squandering time they are most wasteful of the one thing in which it is right to be stingy." – Seneca

OK, let's set the scene....

You're at your desk, ready to get your head down for a productive day. You have targets to meet and a boss to impress - you know the score! A work colleague approaches, takes your wallet off your desk, takes out 20 quid, and walks off without a word. You would be absolutely incensed, apoplectic with rage perhaps, or, at the very least, absolutely miffed! How dare they help themselves to your hard-earned cash!

Now let's set a different scene...

The scenario starts off the same, except this time your work colleague starts asking you about your weekend. You down tools and enter into a lengthy discussion about where you went, who with, and how drunk you got. An hour later he saunters off to his own desk and you pick up where you left off. Are you angry? Annoyed? Probably not.

And why not?

After all, he's probably still just robbed you of 20 quid -in precious time!

Benjamin Franklin said that *"Time is money",* and that's pretty much what Seneca is saying. We guard our money carefully - often to the point of frugality - and yet we don't value our time as much or hold it in such high regard. Which is pretty stupid - we can always earn more money, but we can never earn more time.

It's not just about other people wasting our time either, in fact, that's the least of it. We rob ourselves on a regular and daily basis. We've all felt guilty when we've gone out and spent a lot of money on something - especially if something that end up not being used a few weeks later.

That full gym membership, that ridiculously expensive Nutribullet bought on a whim, when we decide we were going to start 'juicing', those designer shoes that rub your feet and are practically identical to three other (cheaper and more comfortable!) pairs in your wardrobe...

"What a waste of money."

"I worked all week to pay for those, I feel like an idiot."

However, I bet you think nothing of wasting two hours scrolling through your social media feed, looking at nothing in particular and reading the same posts you've already read four hours ago.

Part of the problem is that we believe money is our greatest asset but, spoiler alert, it isn't. Time is. And to be honest, it doesn't really matter how much money you have if you don't have any time to enjoy it.

We all know someone (or perhaps you *are* that someone) who works so hard to earn money, that they haven't enjoyed a family meal since 2001, doesn't get to see their children as much as they'd like, or who hasn't made it to a friend's birthday party for the last five years.

And even for the majority of us, who aren't raking in the big bucks, wasting time simply becomes a mindless habitual activity that we don't even notice is happening - chugging down that morning coffee and dashing off to an uninspiring job, spending our time moaning to colleagues about how much we hate working there, before collapsing on the sofa at the end of the day to sit in front of some crappy TV show like *"Deadenders or Constipation Street!"* while scrolling endlessly through our phones.

What a waste of time when we could be pursuing our goals and dreams, spending time with people we love. Making a difference.

(I have a really great online group called **M**aking **A** **D**ifference, check it out http://Ashtag.team/MAD)

That's not to say that a bit of 'downtime' isn't important...but when it becomes a habit, and we're actively throwing away hours of our time by not spending it productively, it's just downright wasteful. Would you throw handfuls of cash away?

I thought not!

But how can we stop wasting time and start making the most of each day?

Plan Your Day

I'm a big fan of a plan, and not having any kind of plan for your day can lead to the biggest waste of time. Without some idea of what we're doing and when, we can end up drifting aimlessly through the day, just reacting to what comes our way and making no progress towards our goals.

"It's raining, I'll do it tomorrow."

"That'll keep for another day."

"I can't be bothered today."

All legit excuses - at times. But once we put something off once it becomes easy to do it again, and before you know it, it's been a month since we went to the gym, called our grandmother, sent out that CV... We end up in a cycle of inertia, lacking motivation and wasting more and more of our time - and, let's face it - there won't always be a tomorrow.

Time spent on self-improvement, working towards our personal and professional goals, and with our loved ones, is money in the bank of the soul (deep, right?). Setting your alarm early on a Saturday morning and going for a run, or spending a rainy afternoon updating that CV and applying for a job you'll find more inspiring and satisfying than your current one is never wasted time.

So, get yourself a diary or planner, write down your plans for the week and actually follow through and DO them.

Avoid Time Suckers

You'll have to identify yours first, but it's the first step towards making the very most of your precious time.

For a lot of people it's social media. We get sucked into watching other people living their lives and forget to live our own. Perhaps your time sucker is trash TV - fine if that's your guilty pleasure, but try and limit it to an hour a week rather than three hours every night.

It could be that there are people in your life who are time suckers. Those who are constantly draining your time by drawing you into pointless arguments or who love nothing better than to moan about their problems for hours on end with absolutely no intention of doing anything about it.

I'm NOT talking about spending your time listening to friends who need help, advice and support - this is a good use of time...I'm talking about the mate who calls you every night to moan about their job when you've already discussed new career goals with them, helped them write a banging CV and pointed them in the direction of several job openings you've seen online - time sucker!

Listen to them moan, sure, we all do it from time to time - but don't let them (very surmountable) problems become the sole focus of YOUR time.

Maybe it's YOUR job that's the time sucker. You spend so much of your time worrying about it, complaining about it and generally hating it that it leaves precious little time for enjoying life.

In this case a good and productive use of your time would be to find something that DOES inspire you and makes you feel good about yourself - and go for it!

Start Your Day With Intention

This goes hand-in-hand with planning your day, but starting each day with the intention of doing what you planned is a great way to maximise your time.

If you know that today you're going to work-out for an hour, meet an old friend for coffee, and then spend an hour studying for an online course, you know that you're not going to be wasting any time - plus, that's what, three, four hours out of your day? Much more productive than laying on the sofa for three hours staring at Instagram.

Time spent on your health and fitness, your education and on building and maintaining relationships is never wasted - and by making sure you complete your 'objectives' for the day, as dictated by your planner, the positive energy will flow and make you feel that you've had a meaningful day.

It will also inspire you to do the same the next day, and the next and the next.

Feelings of motivation and self-worth will be elevated and your mental health will be boosted. Fact.

Be In A Proactive State

Being in a *reactive* state is the thief of time, allowing outside events to control how you feel and, more importantly, what you do.

Allowing yourself to be consumed by social media, negative news stories, getting involved in pointless arguments or conversations are all symptoms of being in a reactive state.

In order to maximise your time every day you need to make a conscious effort to switch from a reactive state to a proactive state - a state where you start the day with intention and not allow things outside of your control to affect your mood or deviate you from your plans.

The truth is, we don't have a lot of time. Human life is relatively short, and wasting our precious time by drifting aimlessly through our days with no plans or objectives is pretty much like going to the ATM, drawing out your month's wages and chucking it straight in the bin. You couldn't afford to do that and, guess what, you can't afford to throw your precious hours, minutes, and seconds away either.

You can never get them back.

7. UPSET YOU

'You don't have to turn this into something. It doesn't have to upset you. Things can't shape our decisions by themselves' - Marcus Aurelius

Can you *really* choose how to feel? It seems impossible on the surface of it, and yet seems to be what Marcus Aurelius is saying with this famous quote.

But you feel how you feel, surely? No one *chooses* to feel upset, angry, frustrated or stressed, do they?

Perhaps not. But you *can* choose how you deal with that emotion once you have it. You *can* choose to learn from the experience or event that's got you feeling like crap and move forward and adapt. Chances are you've heard (or used) the phrase, 'Don't make a mountain out of a molehill', and that's pretty much saying the same thing - don't let it define you, or put you in a bad mood. Don't sweat the small stuff.

The truth is, you're the only one who has the power over your own mind so, in theory, you can choose to not let the little things bother you, and be happy.

And what do I mean by the 'small stuff'?

You know what I'm talking about - those little day-to-day annoyances that can cast a little dark cloud over your sunny day. Someone drinking the last of the milk before you've had your morning coffee. Someone cutting you up on the motorway. Or queuing for 25 minutes for Costa Coffee during your half hour lunch break.

All things that can seriously piss you off. And I bet you moan about it to everyone who'll listen. After all, getting things off your chest and not bottling it all up is what we're told we should do. And it's true to an extent. AND, when you complain about stuff like this (small things in the grand scheme of it) you're just magnifying the situation and therefore making it bigger than it needs to be and prolonging the bad mood.

Complaining is a mindless habit, and often something we do without thinking. If we're complaining to someone on purpose then it's more often than not just a case of making lazy conversation - and it's a tough habit to change.

We all know someone who does it, don't we? That mate who comes back from a 2 week holiday and instantly goes on about how much it rained the first two days they were there, rather than the amazing food, fantastic beaches, and 4 star accommodation. Or the family member who's first comment when you ask how they enjoyed their meal at a top new restaurant is that they'd run out of his favourite pudding.

If you *don't* know someone like this, it's probably you. And to be honest, in one way or another, it's all of us to some extent. Calling yourself out on this behaviour is the only way to stop it. And when you stop complaining about every little thing - when you stop sweating the small stuff - you'll feel better, and have a more positive effect on those around you.

You can't control the things that happen to you (your train being delayed, your favourite restaurant being fully booked, the shop not stocking those trainers you want in your size...). However, you can control how you act, and the less you let the little things bother you, the happier you will be.

Obviously I'm not saying you should ignore how you feel in every situation, and that you shouldn't stick up for yourself, but you need to learn to choose your battles - or at least make sure there's actually a battle there to fight in the first place!

Chances are, there are bigger things going on that are more worthy of your spent energy than having a bad hair day, shrinking your favourite t-shirt in the tumble drier, or being a few minutes late to an appointment.

And still they bother us, these everyday stressors...and it's not good for us.

Sweating The Small Stuff Can Shorten Our Lifespan

It's not news that being constantly uptight and stressed can make us ill - high blood pressure, heart attacks, strokes etc, are much more likely to be suffered by those who are constantly operating at a high level of stress - and we tend to think of stress caused by death, divorce, or high-powered business stakes when we hear about 'stressed' people keeling over.

So it might surprise you to learn that sweating the small stuff brings the exact same health risks as stress caused by major life events.

An American study showed that people who tend to obsess over little, everyday annoyances live shorter lives than those who just roll with the punches. This is because it's not the *number* of hassles, or even the size of the 'problem' that does you in - it's your perception of whether it's a big deal or not.

Stress - in *any* capacity will take its toll on your health over time, and even if stressing over that broken glass, lost earring, or cancelled concert doesn't induce something as serious as a heart attack, you could still have symptoms like insomnia and a weakened immune system to look forward to eventually.

Something to think about next time the car won't start perhaps.

So, yeah, shit happens - small annoyances are a fact of life, and when we spill something or lose something there can be a split second where it feels like the end of the world. But it's not. The trick is to work out which emotion you feel when small things bother you; is it anger, sadness, frustration? Once you've cracked that, you can consider the following;

Comparing

It's all about putting things into perspective.

Luckily for all the stress-heads out there, humans have the ability to compare a current situation with a past one, and realising that spilling your breakfast down your clean, white shirt 5 minutes before you need to leave the house isn't as stressful as that time you had to give a big presentation at work, for example, can help you to see situations objectively for what they really are.

Is it annoying? Yes. Did you swear? Yes. But do you have a different one you can quickly go and put on? Yes.

Compare the small things that annoy or bother you to past annoyances. The stress from those events passed - and the stress from this one will too.

Throw It Out

I'm a big believer in writing shit down; stuff you want to achieve, stuff you want to change...even the things that annoy you.

Why that last one?

It's been proven that an effective way to get rid of our stressors is by physically throwing them away. So next time you've had a day where the photocopier ran out of paper just as you got there or you forgot your umbrella and it's peeing hard on the walk home, write all the negative thoughts you're having about those situations down on a piece of paper and then screw them up and stick them in the bin.

There's nothing as cathartic as literally chucking away what's stressing you out.

Set A Time Limit

If you absolutely must have a mental rant about something small that's bothered you - set yourself a time limit for it. Give yourself a couple of minutes - 5 tops! - and then move on.

Use those few minutes to really feel and reflect on your emotions, and then make a conscious decision to relax your mind and body, and find a solution to the problem (and not bore your friends or family with complaining over it again!)

Be Mindful

Being 'mindful' might sound like a load of hippy clap-trap, but being aware of your thoughts makes it much easier for you to examine the negative ones before you react to them.

It's this mindfulness that allows you, in effect, to choose how you feel. With practice you'll be able to deflect negative thoughts, or at least approach them in a way that will lead to a more positive outcome for you and those around you.

Reacting before we think is a recipe for making almost any situation worse, but taking stock, thinking about how we feel before we put it all out there, and with any luck changing that negative emotion into something more positive, means we don't have to sweat the small stuff anymore.

8. CONQUER THE WORLD

"Man conquers the world by conquering himself." — *Zeno of Citium*

Like most of the stoic philosophers I've spoken about, Zeno of Citium wasn't telling us anything that isn't obvious when he said this. He's just put it in a grander, fancier-sounding way. Clearly 'conquering the world' isn't to be taken literally (unless you're some sort of movie super-villain), but conquering our 'own' world, ie: becoming successful either personally or professionally, is going to be a hell of a lot easier if we conquer our own demons and weaknesses first.

Health and fitness goals are going to be more achievable if we can conquer our binge-eating/drinking/smoking/laziness 'demons', and conquering the business world will be a cinch if we can conquer weaknesses such as a lack of self-belief, poor motivation, and a tendency to procrastinate.

You get the idea.

And of course, self-improvement is much easier said than done, especially if you don't know where to start.

Perhaps you're not even 100% sure *what* your weaknesses actually are....or perhaps you do, but you've been afraid to admit them for fear of everyone finding out. If you *have* been thinking about starting on the road to self-improvement, chances are you started out by focusing on the negative and being quite hard on yourself.

Actually, you need to be doing the opposite.

The 'be kind' movement's been huge over the last couple of years, and it's much easier to treat other people with kindness and compassion if you've been treating yourself the same way. Self-compassion has been proven to have positive effects on both your physical and mental health

- and if you feel strong and healthy in body and mind, chances are you'll have the mindset to believe you really can conquer the world.

So, let's start small. How can you build self-improvement into your own daily routine, let go of those negative self-thoughts, and conquer them once and for all?

Be Grateful

I'm sure I've banged on about this before at some point, but being consciously grateful can be great for a positive growth mindset.

Keeping a gratitude journal where you write down the things you are thankful for (your family and friends, a job that pays, a capable body, a safe home etc) can reduce stress, improve your relationships with those around you, and even improve your sleep.

And you don't have to think too hard to find things to be grateful for. Just look around you and think about your own life. If you've learnt a new skill, have people around you that enrich your life, have been surprised by a kind deed or favour, or even enjoyed a good book, film or meal recently; then you've got your first few entries right there.

Go Off Grid

Not permanently obviously, but in a world where media (social in particular) is king, the rest of us can often be made to feel inferior.

Everyone's life looks so much more exciting than yours on Facebook, doesn't it? And how about the battering your self-esteem takes when you go online and see that everyone's wearing expensive clothes, going on exotic holidays, and has a body and face that looks like they've been carved by the gods to boot?

Give yourself a digital detox and switch that shit off - even if it's just for a few hours.

Spend that time connecting with your thoughts.

Think about the positive things you have to offer yourself and others. Think about how wonderful your life is, and how you shouldn't compare it or yourself to others, because we are all unique and special.

Positive Self-Talk

You can incorporate this one with your social media break.

Being overly-critical of ourselves and our perceived feelings is common - and a tough one to conquer! Negative self-talk is horribly unproductive and can absolutely smash your motivation to bits. How on earth are you meant to move towards self-improvement if you're constantly telling yourself that you're crap?

Exactly.

Next time you start to feel negative self-thoughts coming, try and nip them in the bud by following it up with something positive. For example, if you feel yourself getting overwhelmed and your mind is full of sentences that start with, 'I can't', tell yourself that, yes, this is a challenge, but you've put lots of work and thought into it and that you're doing the very best you can, and will continue to do so.

The tricky bit is catching the negative thought and making a conscious effort to think differently about the situation. But it's just a case of practice - it will get easier the more you do it.

Be Forgiving

Not just of others, but of yourself too.

Holding onto negative thoughts like regret and resentment is only going to hurt you in the long run. These feelings affect your mood and how you treat yourself and those around you. Make like that awful Disney song and let it go. Practice forgiveness and resolve never to go to bed angry.

Get Enough Sleep

While we're on the subject of bed, not being well-rested and getting enough sleep is going to make you feel shit and unproductive - and no one's conquering anything feeling like that.

Cut down on coffee and alcohol before bed, get into the habit of a good bedtime routine such as a relaxing bath, and practice a bit of meditation before lights out. Good quality sleep is more important than the number of hours, so make sure that you give yourself the best possible chance of a decent rest by resisting the temptation to scroll through social media until the wee small hours, and make your bedroom a relaxing haven.

Practice Self-Care

'Self-care' is definitely one of the buzz phrases of the last couple of years - but it's more than spa treatments and getting your hair done.

Self-care is all about taking the time to look after your own physical, emotional and spiritual needs. Make sure you're getting enough proper nutrition to support your brain and body, exercise to flood your body with feel-good hormones, get outside to de-stress and appreciate nature. Take the time to spend time with people who make you feel valued and happy, and add in some down-time just for you.

If you're thinking, 'and where on earth is work and everything else I have to do meant to factor in with all this self-care', these activities don't have to be time-consuming. A five minute phone call with a mate, a walk around the block, or reading a couple of chapters of a book with a coffee are all forms of self-care that you can fit into your day in no time at all.

Treat Yourself With Kindness

As I mentioned earlier, self-criticism and taking it personally when things go wrong are terribly common and pretty tough to beat.

Human beings have a horrible habit of lingering on stuff that's been said to us - replaying it over and over again and analysing it to bits. Instead of taking everything to heart and allowing it to make us feel shit about ourselves, we should instead think about all the positive ways we impact on the people around us.

If it helps, you can write a list - it doesn't have to be big things, but doing someone a favour or giving someone a compliment can make you feel positive and good about yourself.

Don't beat yourself up over every little thing - let yourself off the hook and remember that tomorrow is another chance to start again. Treat yourself that way you would someone you love - you wouldn't constantly put them down, so don't do it to yourself.

Zeno (The author of this quote) was right; conquering the world really can only be done once you've conquered yourself, so start small; be good to yourself and take one step at a time...and once you believe it, you can achieve it.

9. STUDY THE PAST

'Study the past if you would define the future' - Confucius

Success.

It's what we're all striving for isn't it, whether it's professionally or personally?

The trouble is, success means something different to everyone, and the road to that success is often fraught with challenges and obstacles. It's only natural that along the way we're going to make mistakes, but, hopefully, we can see where we went wrong, and not let them define our future.

For the overwhelming majority, mistakes *are* going to be made on the road to success - and the journey is going to be even more difficult for us if we keep repeating the same ones over and over again.

So, how do we avoid it? How can we make sure that it's *learning* from our mistakes that define our future success, rather than letting those mistakes cast a shadow over it?

They say that history is doomed to repeat itself - but that doesn't have to be the case.

We only repeat our past mistakes if we haven't learned our lesson yet. Having a growth mindset will give you the ability to learn from your past, behave differently, and make wiser decisions. Making a mistake is fine; it happens, to everyone and in all walks of life - but what strategies can we put in place to avoid making the same mistake twice..?

Awareness precedes change!

Recognise It

Recognising the mistake in the first place is step one.

In some cases you might recognise it straight away, in other instances you won't - but just *knowing* that you made one will help avoid making it again.

Most of the time you'll be able to work backwards and identify the decision that led you there - but only if you keep that positive, growth-set mindset in place, rather than weeping and wailing and thinking that all is lost.

So; notice it, own it...then think about doing something about it.

Forgive Yourself

Beating yourself up when you make a mistake is pointless - what's done is done, all you can do is learn from the experience.

Some people might scoff and say this is 'letting yourself off the hook' - and in effect, you are!

But why bloody not?

In real life, a lot of your endeavours might fail at first, and for more reasons than you can count; timing, a lack of adequate skills or resources, lack of motivation, poor execution...

But you're not alone, and, more importantly, 'failure' isn't a dirty word - it just means you tried something and it didn't work out.

Sure, the consequences of failing at something could be annoying, difficult - even life-changing - but you have to forgive yourself in order to move forward.

Be kind to yourself, and try again.

Visualise Successful Resolution

OK, so you made a mistake.

Take a deep breath and visualise your end goal. What is it you're trying to work towards? What do you want? What are you aiming to achieve? Once you've reaffirmed that, you can get yourself back on track.

If you find visualisation tricky, you could write your goals down instead. It's an idea not to get *too* attached to your idea of success though - your circumstances might change, your knowledge might grow and you might have new experiences that take you in another direction.

This might even be as a direct result of the mistake, so embrace it and keep going - you could end up with a different, but better, end result!

Work out How You Got To The Mistake

Once you've identified that something was a mistake, and you know that you don't want to make it again, you'll need to retrace your steps backwards to work out how you got there in the first place.

In hindsight, are there any decisions you made when you started pursuing success that stand out now as 'bad'?

On the flip-side, what GOOD decisions did you make that you DON'T want to change?

Was it a lack of knowledge or information that led you to make a mistake? Was your goal too big - or too small? Did any external factors play a part? Is there anything you could have put in place that would have lessened the impact of a mistake?

Once you've worked that out, you'll be able to work out what changes you need to make to ensure it doesn't happen again.

Repeat Positive Behaviours Until They Become A Habit

You can beat your repeated 'bad behaviours' that lead you to make mistakes, by making a conscious effort to repeat positive ones instead.

Are you someone who jumps in both feet first? Are you impulsive? Are you a person who doesn't do the research before taking action?

These bad habits are a recipe for making the same mistake more than once. Make being organised and prepared your newest habits by practicing them over and over again. Make lists of pros and cons before you make a decision. Study, and consider all possibilities from every angle.

It sounds like a lot of work - but it will save you time and effort in the long run when you don't have to recover from another mistake

Making a well-thought out and informed decision means you're less likely to make the same mistake you have in the past.

Focus On What Goes Right, Not On What Goes Wrong

Easier said than done when you've made what you consider to be a monumental mistake - but if you spend your energy focusing on the things you've done wrong it makes it more likely that more 'wrong' will follow.

I'm not saying don't take a look at what led to the mistake, or what you can do to ensure it doesn't happen again (these are positive steps you can take). Just don't spend your time and effort dwelling on it and lamenting your bad fortune.

Take away your mistake's power by focusing on the things you've done right, and let that positive energy move you forwards in the right direction.

So, when it comes to recovering mistakes, there's a lot to be said for recognising what's gone wrong, learning a lesson from it, and adjusting your mindset to one of growth and positivity in order to not make the same mistake again.

Not repeating the mistakes from our past so they don't define our future success really does have an awful lot to do with the habits we build. Obviously we don't *want* to make mistakes, so it can be particularly frustrating when we make the same one more than once.

But *why* does that have a tendency to happen? Surely it's not just bad luck or 'one of those things'...?

Well, here comes the science bit...

It's all to do with neural pathways that are created every time we do something, good or bad.

This is basically how habits are created; so when we make a mistake we are simply slipping by default into an existing pathway of a 'bad habit'.

Perhaps this is the reason why someone might have had five or six failing businesses, or why you always attract the wrong sort of partner, for example - you're just treading a well-worn habitual path.

Interestingly this is the exact same phenomenon that means you can't find your keys even though they are right there in front of your face where you always leave them, and also the reason for 'tip of the tongue syndrome': you KNOW the right word, but you just can't 'find' it, and then when you do it's such a relief that you can't imagine ever forgetting it again. But of course, you will - it's become a habit.

This is why it's so much more productive to look at what you want to achieve from a different angle, and make THAT a habit, rather than trying the same thing over and over again. The M.I.S.T.A.K.E Method teaches us to avoid revisiting past mistakes in an effort not to repeat them.

Make A List

I've briefly mentioned making lists already, but really get into the habit of writing down behaviours that you want to change.

This could be lifestyle stuff - smoking, drinking, gambling, overeating, overspending, etc, or business practices, the way you parent, the way you conduct yourself in a relationship...anything that you think leads you to making mistakes.

Identify Your Triggers

When you look at your list do you see any patterns or triggers that are causing you to make the same mistakes more than once?

Perhaps it's the company you keep, the hours you work, or what you do for a living, for example.

I'm not talking here about placing blame - you are an adult in charge of your own decisions and destiny - but identifying patterns can help you make positive changes that could stop you repeating your past mistakes.

Switch Your Routine

Now it's time to make those changes, and sometimes it's a simple case of switching up our routine in order to avoid repeating our mistakes.

Perhaps you binge-eat (undoing all of your hard work at the gym) when you binge-watch your favourite show on Netflix. So limit your viewing now that you've identified that as a trigger.

Maybe you gamble more than you can afford to lose when you hang out with Bob - so maybe knock Bob on the head for a while (figuratively speaking).

Trade Old Habits For New Ones

So, if you're going to switch your routine - you have to actually switch it! Don't just stop eating in front of the TV or heading off to the bookies three nights a week - replace it with something else.

Hang out with a different friend, swap snacking for knitting (you get the idea). If you don't fill the void with something else you're just going to end up going back to the behaviours that lead you to make mistakes.

Accept That You're Not Perfect

While it's true that you want to set new standards for yourself, what you're aiming for is improvement, not perfection. Expecting perfection just isn't realistic.

When you start making changes, you'll still make the odd mistake. And that's OK; you're still a human being, albeit a human being who is trying to make some positive changes.

Key Strengths

During your journey of self-improvement be sure to focus on your strengths rather than your weaknesses. Concentrating on your faults only makes you less likely to succeed.

Focusing on the negative makes us see more mistakes that we could make in the future, and fills us with self-doubt and the fear of failure. Instead, put all of your energy into your positive attributes, your skills and talents - you can use these to make positive life changes.

End The Self-Sabotage

This is really just an extension of focusing on your key strengths - our fear of failure and rejection is often what causes us to self-sabotage the task at hand.

It also breeds procrastination because we become too scared to even *start* working towards our goals.

You've heard of 'failing before you start because you fail to start' - yeah, that's what that is.

Either that or we give up before we've reached our goals and end up sliding back into our old behaviour because it feels familiar and 'safe'. (Also referred to as 'Snap Back')

We have to break the cycle - otherwise we really are doomed to repeat our mistakes and let them define our future.

<u>M</u>ake A List

<u>I</u>dentify Your Triggers

<u>S</u>witch Your Routine

<u>T</u>rade Old Habits For New Ones

<u>A</u>ccept That You're Not Perfect

<u>K</u>ey Strengths

<u>E</u>nd The Self-sabotage

10 FOLLOW THE HERD

"We should not, like sheep, follow the herd of creatures in front of us, making our way where others go, not where we ought to go." — Seneca

'If you can dream it you can do it!'

'Follow your dreams!'

'Just do you!'

All very motivating and encouraging, and just a very small sample of the types of quote that are rooted in Seneca's stoicism. I'm pretty sure that a simple five minute search on Instagram or Pinterest will serve up a million more. All telling you the same thing in an around about way, namely 'don't worry about what everyone else is doing; follow your own path'.

The trouble is, that sometimes, following our own path isn't as simple as a flowery internet quote or cheesy wall decal would have you believe.

Sometimes, living the life we want to live can be littered with obstacles. Following our own path might mean making choices that go against the expectations of our families and friends, our communities...maybe even our culture or religion. In turn this can lead to us facing isolation, stigma...or at the very least a sigh and an eye-roll from our parents and mates as we embark on what they might consider to be a wasted journey.

So, should we still take the road less travelled? Even if it's not where others think we ought to be going? Fuck yeah!

Sure, it might not be a smooth path; you're likely to trip and fall at least once, and you're bound to hear 'I told you so' a couple of times, but you only get one life. Why spend it travelling somewhere you don't want to go when, as Fleetwood Mac said, "you can go your own way"?

What are some of the advantages of following your own path?

We End Up Having Less Fear Of Failure

After all, no decision we make in life is risk-free, and carving a new path for ourselves is going to involve a lot of trial and error, and probably holds quite a lot of potential for error.

AND, experiencing failure more often can actually help us to view it as a learning opportunity and a chance to grow - rather than seeing it as a slight on our abilities.

This growth mindset makes success a lot more likely.

We Develop A Thicker Skin

It's not a nice feeling when someone is disappointed in you, or judgmental or disapproving of your choices. It might even be enough to put you off following your chosen path altogether.

And you'll soon come to realise that people's reactions to the way you want to live your life comes less from what they really think about us, and has more to do with their own fears and insecurities, and often - their own jealousy!

Perhaps they're someone who never followed their dreams, and instead took the path they thought they *should* rather than the one they *wanted*. Now they're stuck in a job they don't particularly like, living a lifestyle they don't particularly enjoy...and seeing you all hyped-up about travelling the world, or becoming an artist, or starting a llama farm has them feeling all sorts of envy and regret!

Try looking at it from that point of view, rather than feeling upset that they seem disappointed in you, or are scoffing at your idea. You'll find you won't take the hurtful comments as personally, and you might even feel some empathy for them.

It Gives You The Freedom To Be Who You Really Are

There's nothing *wrong* with what we might call a 'conventional' lifestyle. A 9-5 job, perhaps marriage and children, buying a house in a family-friendly neighbourhood, decent car, pub on a Friday, a week abroad once a year, golf on Saturdays, boot fairs on Sundays…. This is an aspirational lifestyle for many, and a path that many walk down willingly, knowing exactly where they're going and that it's exactly what they want.

And good for them. They are being authentic and true to themselves.

Lifestyles are not a one-size-fits all deal, and if you don't live the life that aligns with who you really are, you can suffer psychologically.

Research has shown that being able to express yourself authentically is vital to our mental well-being. Even if it means losing friends or acquaintances along the way, you owe it to YOU to be true to yourself.

We should listen to the opinions of friends and family, shouldn't we? Surely they have our best interests at heart - especially our parents.

If they think that university is a must, then perhaps we should go…your dad's always dreamt of you following in his footsteps and becoming a paramedic - and he loves his job, so surely you will too…your mum would love to see you settle down and marry, have a couple of kids and live in domestic bliss like she did; and why not? She seems very happy with that life.

It can be quite tempting to have your important life decisions influenced and determined by other people. It frees you from the responsibility of making your own decisions and, in part, your own mistakes. If it all goes tits-up it's not your fault, you didn't want to do it in the first place! Right?

However, if you don't follow your own path, and let other people decide how you should live your life, you'll end up regretting it.

Even if that decision is made by those who gave you that life in the first place! Letting other people decide your path isn't the same as asking for advice or an objective opinion from a trusted source, don't forget.

When you do that it can help you to make a decision, sure, but ultimately the onus is still on you and you alone to make that decision. You *might* make one that you regret, sure, but you're much more likely to be haunted by that decision if it wasn't one that you made yourself.

Let's not pretend that following your own path is always the easiest option.

It's not just those closest to us who'll have an opinion on how you choose to live your life - society as a whole tends to have a very narrow and specific view on what constitutes a 'successful' life. As a rule society tells us that successful people make a lot of money. They live in nice (preferably big) houses in 'good' neighbourhoods and drive nice cars. They're married with a couple of kids and have stable, well-paid, 'proper' jobs. Which to many people is their idea of a successful life.

And that *is* a lot of people's idea of a successful life - perhaps it's what you aspire to, or even already have.

That view of success doesn't constitute a successful life for everyone. A lot of people simply don't fit into the 'married-with-a-couple-of-kids-and-living-in-a-big-house' mould. And even worse than that - this very pervasive definition can often lead to people making huge life decisions that end up being mistakes!

Think about all those people who get married because that's what society expects of them, only to discover that a married lifestyle isn't really for them. Or people who have children for the same reason, without having the desire or disposition to raise a family, and who end up sending unhappy people out into the world.

If you want to live your happiest, most successful life according to YOU, then ignore society's definition of success and stop worrying about what other people will think.

If you are confident in the life choices you make, and you set off down your own path, life will suddenly flow. Not saying there won't be anything to trip you up along the way, but it will still be a smoother path than if you'd taken the one that was wrong for you.

This is because you'll be living a life that matches your personality and skills and not stressing about trying to achieve what everyone else wants you to achieve. You'll be living an authentic life instead of following the herd and you'll be happier than you ever imagined.

11. ACTION STEPS

'When it is obvious that the goals cannot be reached, don't adjust the goals; adjust the action steps.' - Confucius

In a nutshell - when the going gets tough, don't give up! Don't just give up on your hopes and dreams (read: goals). Simply change your mindset, re-evaluate the situation, and come up with a new strategy.

This quote is basically all about coming up with a better plan when something gets in the way of where we're going, rather than just chucking the towel in.

Easier said than done sometimes though, isn't it.

Working towards something we want can be exhausting - whether it's something relating to a new business, building a better relationship, working towards becoming a homeowner, or starting on a new career path.

These will always be days where you think, 'bugger this, it's too hard, I'm never going to make it', and if that situation sounds familiar, remembering this quote from Confucius could help you get back on track.

Take a step back, a deep breath and try to figure out why you're not getting to where you want to go as quickly or as smoothly as you want. Instead of setting a closer or 'easier' goal, you need to adjust your action steps.

Giving up and moaning about it is easy - but where's the reward? (spoiler alert: there isn't one)...Putting in time and effort can be hard, but the rewards are great. Look for a more efficient path, adjust your attitude and start walking!

'Sounds good', I hear your cry, 'fancy giving us some tips?'

Well, as luck would have it....

Consistency Is Key

Whatever your goals are in life; getting that business off the ground, saving money, losing weight, finding a better career....something that goes hand in hand with a positive, growth mindset, and that will make all the difference when it comes to achieving what you want, is consistency.

Consistency is mainly about staying focused on your goals and being really committed to achieving them. But it's not something that comes easy to everyone - and it's not as simple as *just* constantly visualising where you want to be - you HAVE to put in the work in order to make it happen.

Why is it that so many of us find it hard to be consistent?

I'm sure you've been there; let's say you want to be a writer. You've already visualised yourself signing the 6-figure book deal and you know who you would want to play your main protagonist in the blockbuster movie adaptation, now if only you could knuckle down and write the 2,000 words a day you promised yourself you would.

Or let's say you want to lose weight. You've set yourself a training schedule, you've got a meal plan, and there's more lycra in your wardrobe than an Olympic cyclist.

But....after a few days of consistency you start struggling to remember exactly what it is you're meant to be doing each day. You got side-tracked today, so you'll start again tomorrow. Your mate called and asked you to go for a beer after work....you had a shit day at the office...you start finding it harder and harder to get motivated.

Maybe you'll start again Monday. Or at the beginning of next month. Before you know it, days have passed since you thought about your goals, and weeks since you looked at your schedule or set foot in the gym, or switched on your laptop.

No one's saying that you have to become an overnight success, but if you don't take the steps towards your goals and, more importantly, *keep going*, you're never going to get there.

Now, the truth is that something like weight loss CAN be achieved if you're not very consistent - but it'll take you a hell of a lot longer if you go to the gym once a week and eat well 3 days out of 7, than if you work out every other day and eat well all week.

The same goes for learning a new skill such as another language or an instrument. Being consistent is going to help you to achieve your goal faster AND make it less likely that you'll give up because you're not seeing results as quickly as you'd like.

The good news is that you can actually train yourself to have self-discipline and be consistent - and it's going to help you massively!

The Benefits Of Consistency

First and foremost, consistency is good for your mental health.

The human brain likes routine; there is a certain comfort in knowing what's happening and when, and a satisfaction that comes from following a plan.

People who consistently follow a schedule for working out, learning, training etc feel less stressed and more at ease than those who lurch from day to day unsure whether they'll be going to the gym today or reading another chapter of that textbook.

When you have a consistent routine for working towards your goals it becomes a habit, allowing your brain to enter an 'autopilot' mode. That means that more energy can be dedicated to other stuff. You'll also feel a sense of accomplishment when you commit to a schedule, which can give a real boost to your sense of self-worth.

All in all, working consistently towards your goals is great for your mental wellbeing.

Training Yourself To Be Consistent

The first step, as with many things, is recognising that you want to change. Tell yourself that you WANT to be more consistent - if you don't *really* want to make a change, you're going to struggle to make it happen.

So, what tools and techniques can you use to help you stay consistent and keep on the path towards your goals?

Technology

We all use technology every day - it's become our norm. It's how we work, how we communicate, and often how we socialise. It can also help us to be more consistent when it comes to achieving our goals.

You can now download goal-tracking apps to your phone or tablet that allow you to set goals and log your progress as you work towards them. Habit-building apps do a similar thing, and they're available for practically any element of your life that you want to improve.

You can track your calorie intake, water intake, the amount of sleep you're getting, how many steps you take….you're bound to find one relating to your specific goal that will be able to help you stay consistent and on track.

And it's not just tracking your progress that you can do through your phone. Want to learn something new? There's an app for that too. If your goal is to learn a new skill - a language, a craft, or even how to meditate - there are apps that not only track your progress, but that guide you through how to achieve your goal as well through instructional guides.

Technology means it's never been easier to track how we're getting on with something...and it's much easier to stay consistent if you've got little reminders pinging up every day!

Good Old Pen And Paper

Perhaps you're more of an old-fashioned guy or gal and apps really aren't your style. Keeping a progress diary or journal will do the job just as well, and satisfy your thirst for putting pen to paper at the same time.

Tracking your habits by writing down how you're doing and when you're doing it serves the same purpose as doing it through an app. It's visual proof of your hard work and how far you've come, and, much like with the apps, tracking your progress every day will motivate you to get started because you won't want to break your streak and lose your progress!

Of course, there'll be no reminder automatically popping up daily on your phone in order to keep you consistent if you're using pen and paper - so you'll either have to set yourself one, or keep your dairy/journal in a place where you're going to see it every day and be reminded that you need to write in it - next to the kettle for example!

Use Visual Reminders

If you want to be more consistent in working your way towards your goals then you need to keep those dreams front and centre.

Make a visualisation board and keep it in your bedroom so it's the first thing you look at every morning. It can be incredibly motivating to wake up and instantly see a pic of your dream home, dream body, or dream holiday destination!

Write motivational quotes on post-it notes and leave them around the house. The bathroom mirror or the fridge are handy locations...this will keep your focus on your goals as you go about your daily routine.

Focus On The Process - Not Just The Goal

I've spoken a lot about keeping focused on your goal - and of course if you want to achieve it you need to be committed to getting there. But focusing on the actual process of staying consistent is just as important (if not more so!) than focusing on the goal itself.

Sometimes, if we focus just on our goal, we can start to feel discouraged at how far away it feels, which can be disheartening. If we put our effort and focus into *reaching* the goal instead, it can be incredibly motivating.

Squash Self-Doubt

Self-doubt makes us our own worst enemy when it comes to sabotaging ourselves - including when it comes to being consistent in working towards our goals.

If you embrace a growth mindset and a positive 'can-do' attitude, it's going to make all the difference when it comes to staying consistent.

The second you tell yourself you can't do something, you're going to struggle. If you know that you CAN achieve that goal, then much of the hard work is already done.

You're not going to achieve your goals overnight, but that's OK. When there's an obstacle in your way, change tactics and start again. Keep perspective, focus, have a plan, and be consistent - and you'll get there.

12. FOOLISH ONE

"We must not say that every mistake is a foolish one." – Marcus Tullius Cicero

Natural disasters...decaffeinated coffee....making mistakes....all bad things, right?

Two out of three for sure, but mistakes? Not as much as we might think.

And yet, for the most part, the thought of making a mistake is terrifying. What will people think? What will your colleagues or boss think? A mistake could cost you your relationship, your job, or your business. Certainly scary stuff.

Cicero says, not every mistake we make is necessarily a bad thing. The fear of making mistakes can be paralysing, stopping you from trying anything new or moving out of your comfort zone. We make mistakes from childhood - it's how we learn to read, write, ride a bike, make friends...our teenage and young adult years are littered with mistakes - financial, romantic, personal... And then as we get older - mistakes on our chosen career path, mistakes if we start our own businesses...it goes on and on.

A mistake is just a lesson, and you can't grow if you don't allow yourself to make them. All we can really do is focus on what we learn from it and how to improve from it. Don't keep beating yourself over the head with it just because you messed up. You just need to recognise that you simply made a mistake - dwelling on it and agonising over it isn't going to change the fact that it happened.

And it doesn't mean you're a failure because you made a mistake - you and the mistake are not the same thing at all.

With any luck you learned something valuable from it and can now move onwards and just get on with things.

Focusing on an actual solution and, who knows, probably end up further ahead than if you'd never allowed yourself to make the mistake in the first place.

(I hope you're enjoying the pep-talk so far)

I know we're talking about what Cicero said, but Thomas Edison also got in there with, "I have not failed. I've just found 10,000 ways that won't work."

Wise words.

In fact, a light bulb's probably just gone off and you've realised (perhaps for the first time), that a lot of the times, they're not even *really* mistakes. You just learned that a different strategy was needed - you found a different way. As with most things, how you deal with a perceived mistake is down to mindset; don't think of mistakes as failures, think of them as feedback. Embrace the additional knowledge you now have as a result of that 'mistake'

Better that than thinking, 'what if', if nothing else at least!

Questions such as, What if I'd tried? What if I'd said something? What if I'd taken that new job?....are much scarier than the idea that something might be a mistake. Don't regret the things you do, regret the things you don't do, as they say.

Human beings are weird creatures, because often the fear of making a mistake doesn't even really come from worrying about the consequences of the action. It comes from the world's most fruitless question: "What will people think?"

Spoiler alert: most people don't even notice or even *care*, much less actually judge you for any mistake you might make - certainly not anywhere near as much as we think they do.

And to be honest, if you gain something from it, knowledge about yourself or the situation for example, why let the fear of what someone else might think stop you?

Fuck 'em. You can never really know what someone else is thinking anyway, so don't let it stop you from doing the things that you want to do. And anyway, you never know, they might even be really impressed at your willingness to take a chance and try new things rather than thinking, 'oh my god, what a useless twat.'

You just don't know. You can only know what **you're** thinking - which, granted, is sometimes a bit annoying.

The truth is, even if there are witnesses to your mistakes who might be rolling their eyes or sniggering about it behind your back. Much more important than their judgement is understanding what you now know about yourself.

Blowing it could actually give you valuable insight you probably couldn't have got any other way; insight that makes you more comfortable with yourself and helps you move forward in a more confident way.

After all, we're all just trying to do our best and we make mistakes sometimes, that's just life. But having the mindset that any mistake is a learning experience is only going to come back to you in good ways. In fact, people are much more likely to trust and respect you for being comfortable enough with yourself to make, embrace, and learn from your mistakes.

Basically, we all fuck up sometimes (me more than most!) It happens - and if we didn't make any mistakes we wouldn't learn anything or grow. Of course that's an easy thing to say, and for a lot of us that fear of stuffing things up can have a huge impact, with us only focusing on the things that go wrong and not being able to bounce back from it.

If that sounds like you, you'll be glad to know that there are some ways you can retrain your brain and turn it around.

You Just Have To Accept It

Easier said than done, yes, but if you make a mistake, the first thing to get into your head is that you are NOT your mistake. It doesn't define you as a person. If you've got that little voice in your head telling you that you're a screw-up, tell it to do one.

Yeah, you might have screwed up, but take a deep breath and keep in mind that something valuable might yet come from it - it doesn't have to be the finished article.

Don't start jumping to conclusions about your worth or value. No one's perfect, and that's OK. Normal even. Yep, it happened...now to work out how to move on from it.

Own It

Once you've accepted your mistake head-on, own what happened and draw a line under it.

It might be tempting to look for an easy out and blame someone else instead of owning it yourself. So if thoughts along the lines of; 'That was her fault, she's always had it in for me' start creeping in, get shot of them.

Admitting to yourself that you're the one at fault is the first step towards getting back on track. If you're making excuses for yourself and blaming other people, you're just stopping yourself from moving forward.

Work Out Where You Went Wrong

Most of the time when we make a mistake it's fairly obvious where we went wrong. However, sometimes you might be confused about where you went wrong, which can make it really tricky to put it in the past. You're more likely to dwell on something if it's bugging the crap out of you!

Don't forget that your mindset plays a huge part in how you view and react to the mistakes that you make. A growth mindset will see mistakes as an opportunity to improve….a fixed mindset will see them as something you are doomed to repeat. Which mindset you have is down to you and you alone.

Have A Go At Fixing It

Most problems have a solution, so if you've made a mistake somewhere along the line, sit down and think about what you can do to improve the situation.

It could be that it's not as bad as you initially thought and there are things that you can do to smooth things over. This is where a growth mindset is going to be invaluable!

Talk It Out

When you make a really big mistake, don't feel that you have to cope with it on your own.

Talk it out with someone - a friend or family member. They might come up with a solution you haven't thought of or be able to offer some support. At the very least it might be nice to have someone to have a little whinge to before moving past it and cracking on.

'There are no mistakes, only lessons' - sounds like one of those nauseating insta-quotes, doesn't it? But, when you really stop to think, it really is a pretty strong message.

Everyone will make a mistake at some point, and everyone has to deal with them. It's how you pick yourself up from it and move forward that counts Start to see mistakes as opportunities, a chance to pick up a little extra knowledge and improve yourself and your way of doing things along the way. And remember the words of Cicero; mistakes aren't foolish, they are merely a way of gaining experience, growing and pushing forward - it's how we deal with them that defines us.

13. WHAT YOU WOULD BE

'First say to yourself what you would be; and then do what you have to do - Epictetus

A pretty self-explanatory quote I reckon - no hidden meaning there! Work out what you want, and then do whatever it takes to get there. It's pretty much a quote about determination - about not being all talk and no action.

And it's the 'say to yourself' bit that I really want to focus on.

How many times have you thought to yourself that you need to get a new job/start that business/join that gym/redecorate the downstairs loo?

Exactly!

Doesn't necessarily mean you've taken the steps to get to where you want to be, does it?

Would it make a difference if you said it out loud?

Before you scoff and say, 'no, of course not', you might be interested to know that in fact, research shows that people who speak their goals out loud, are more likely to achieve them. I'm not talking about a public declaration - in fact, that can sometimes have the opposite effect - I'm talking about _saying_ it to yourself, rather than just thinking it.

Call it what you will; affirmations, manifestation, magick, cosmic ordering, praying -putting the words 'out there', into the universe where you can hear them, is often the first step to getting to where you want to be.

Now, before you dismiss this as a load of hocus-pocus, mumbo-jumbo, hear me out.

This is about a mindset, not a magical, mystical belief system - even those who subscribe to cosmic ordering or money-magick etc don't believe that there's a genie in the sky ready and waiting to grant all of their wishes.

They appreciate that there's some effort involved on their part. If you ask the universe for the job of your dreams, it's unlikely to land on your lap if you don't start applying, updating your CV, learning new skills...

Saying it out loud gives you the motivation to start taking the steps towards getting the job that you want, and there's a hell of a lot to be said for having a positive mindset and believing in yourself. In that respect, you will get back what you put out there.

Let's take a look at pro athletes as an example...positive affirmations and visualisation plays a huge part in their training and prep. They visualise themselves making great shots, running faster, performing better...they 'big themselves up' - either in private, or even publicly (boxers, I'm looking at you).

No athlete, striving to be at the top of their game, to win gold, to be a champion, is going to go into any event or competition with anything other than a positive mindset...because they know that as soon as any self-doubt comes creeping in, they're knackered.

And the same might go for you as well! If you go into a job interview and your overriding thought is, 'I'm not going to get this job", then it's likely you won't - not because of any 'magic', but because it becomes a self-fulfilling prophecy. You'll be so preoccupied with that negative thought that you'll fudge your answers, not smile, not relax or come across as a positive person, and basically sabotage yourself.

Now, I'm not saying that if you go in there thinking you're going to boss the interview that you absolutely will, but going in there with confidence, *knowing* that you could do the job well, open, receptive, and positive, you're much more likely to come across as exuding the qualities they're looking for in an employee.

I said earlier that taking your self-talk from a silent thought to an out-loud, verbal one has been found to motivate you and move you forward with your goals - and it's true.

Here comes the science bit....

There have been several studies that suggest articulating what you want to be out loud helps you to focus on the goal and the journey towards it, as well as helping you to squash self-doubt and self-criticism - the death toll to many a personal hope and dream!

This phenomenon is known as 'feedback hypothesis' and there have been several experiments undertaken in order to prove that it exists.

In one study, participants had to look through a stack of photographs and look for one of a specified object. Those who said the name of the object they were looking for out loud whilst looking through the pictures, found it faster than those who didn't.

Another study was done on athletes; basketball players who spoke motivational affirmations out loud as they played ("I can.." type statements), performed better than those players who just stayed silent.

You've probably done it yourself without even thinking about it. Ever been driving around aimlessly looking for a parking space, and as soon as you say out loud, 'oh please let there be a bloody space!' you suddenly spot one?

Thought so.

Saying it out loud, whatever it is - something you're trying to find, an aim, or a goal, makes it 'real' and creates a positive reinforcement of the action you're taking. When you choose to focus your attention on a specific idea it makes it easier to focus on YOU.

Now the kicker - *thinking* about speaking your intentions out loud is one thing, *doing* it is quite another.

It can feel a bit awkward at first and might make you feel like a bit of a twat, for want of a better word. But here are some tips that might help.

Find Your Own Space

I'm not suggesting you start vocalising your positive affirmations on the bus or in the supermarket (you might get dragged off by the men in white coats), but finding somewhere private and secure - your bedroom, your bathroom, a quiet outdoor area where you can be alone - will help you to break the ice with yourself.

You probably will still feel a bit stupid at first, but with practice and in the comfort of a safe space, you'll soon get the hang of it.

Work Out Exactly What You're Going To Say

'I want a new job' or 'I want to earn more money' are very vague - how can you start taking the steps to achieve what you want without being more specific. Expressing out loud the exact job you want, the type of salary you want to earn, or your goal weight, will make it easier to work towards.

If you're not feeling confident enough to start making those demands of yourself, begin by being kind to yourself and repeating positive affirmations. It can help if you look in a mirror as you say it. 'I am worthy', 'I deserve to earn more money', 'I would excel in that line of work'...these types of positive phrases will bolster your confidence over time and give you the self-belief you need to start applying for higher-paying positions or changing your career path.

Change HOW You Say It

Tiny changes in the way you speak to yourself can really increase your words' positive power! Try addressing yourself in the second or third person:

'*You* deserve to earn more'

'*Bob* is worth it'

It might make you feel a bit nuts, but using your own name, or using 'you', can help you see things from a distance. This new perspective can be really helpful in changing any negative self-talk. After all, it's always much easier to say that someone else deserves something or is good at something than it is to say 'I am...'

Using your own name can make it much easier to be positive about getting to where you want to be. It's not always easy to think of yourself as deserving of good things - especially if you struggle with self-confidence and self-doubt...but Bob? Bob deserves the world! Bob is a stand-up guy who would absolutely smash that new job! Go Bob!

Do It Every Day!

Once you've done it once, being consistent is key. Make saying your aims and goals out loud a daily habit. Start every morning with positive affirmations to motivate you to drive your day forward and move closer towards who and what you want to be.

Talking to yourself is not often encouraged (although often it's your only hope of an intelligent conversation), so it might take some practice - and you might get some weird looks as it becomes more normal for you and you graduate from the bathroom mirror to the morning commute, whilst sat at your desk, or whilst going for your morning walk.

And, saying out loud what you need to hear on a regular basis can be one of the most positive, motivating steps you can take towards your future....because after that, all you need to do is, (as Epictetus would say). 'do what you have to do.'

14. DON'T EXPLAIN

'Don't explain your philosophy, embody it' - Epictetus

Let the results speak for themselves.

Actions, not words.

Show them, don't tell them.

Or, as Nike are fond of saying - just do it!

I think that's pretty much what Epictetus was trying to say when he came up with this timeless quote. And surely that goes against a lot of what we're taught when it comes down to reaching our goals and targets?

For a lot of people, making a public declaration of what they're going to do - whether that be giving up smoking, pursuing a new career or reaching a new fitness goal - makes them feel that they have more chance of achieving it.

And that makes sense.

After all, once you've announced it to your family, or written it on Facebook, or made a Tik Tok about it - you will want your audience to see it through to the end. Right? I mean, there's nothing like the fear of being in the chippy and someone tapping you on the shoulder to say, 'Hey, I thought you were on a diet?' to keep you motivated is there? With your peers to hold you accountable, how can you ever fail to run that marathon, write that novel, or shift those pounds?

The thought behind this is that no one likes to feel like a failure, do they? You don't want to let anyone down or disappoint them, so surely the more people you share your plans with the better - lots of people to motivate you, keep you on track, and either have a go at you or take the piss when you fall on your arse and quit.

However, If you're only working towards your goal through fear of what other people might think or say, or you're just trying to achieve it for someone else, then your heart won't really be in it and your victory will be lacklustre.....and that's if you even get there at all.

And why wouldn't you get there?

People KNOW, you've SAID what you're going to do - it has been set in stone and therefore it shall be done. Except that by telling everyone what you're up to you've put yourself under a lot of pressure and set yourself up for a pretty big fall if you do fail - something *no one* wants an audience for.

Let's take 'improving fitness' as an example goal. You've bought all the gear and joined the gym. You've worked out a killer schedule and routine that will have you looking buff in no time, you've got one of those shaker cups for your protein shake.....You've even practiced your selfie poses ready for the 'gram. It's all over your social media - starting Monday, it is ON!!! And it starts off well; you're working out 5 times a week, you're only consuming green stuff and water, and your 'likes' on Facebook are through the roof!

Then, a few weeks in, for whatever reason, you miss a session. Then another. Then another. Not a big deal - work, social life, illness, etc, it all gets in the way at some point or another, and if you hadn't told the world and his wife that you were going to be absolutely shredded by the summer, there wouldn't be an issue.

You'd chalk this blip up to 'one of those things' and then get back to working towards your goal tomorrow. No big deal - you fall off the horse, you get back on and all that.

However, you've told anyone who will listen that the gym is now life, so it's not long before the comments start....

"Thought you'd be at the gym."

"Is that a burger and chips I can see in your Snapchat?"

" That didn't last long did it!?"

And now you feel like crap.

Whether the comments come from general disappointment for you, or whether there's an element of smugness and 'I told you so' about it, failing publicly is never going to make you feel great, and it might even absolutely kill your motivation stone dead - I mean, you're not going to attempt it *again* are you?

Well, you can - and you should. Except this time, keep it to yourself. Scientific research has actually shown that if you really want to reach that dream or goal - you need to keep schtum.

And there are 3 main reasons why....

Premature Praise

This is exactly what it sounds like; the second you tell someone that you're going to write a novel, for example, you'll probably get a lot of, 'Oh you clever thing! I wish I could do something like that!' type comments. And it'll feel good. You're already getting praise for doing something you haven't even done yet - and it's addictive.

The more people you tell, the more 'good for you!' style comments you're going to get - and it's unlikely that you'll get that same 'high', even when you've completed your novel/lost that weight/got that job.

This could be part and parcel of why sharing your goal publicly can make you less likely to do the work to actually achieve it - you've already received the bit that makes your brain release all of those lovely chemicals which mean you feel great, without having to do any of the hard work.

In a world where everyone wants instant gratification and we're constantly seeking approval from family, friends and strangers alike online, you can see why this happens so often. If you have a goal - particularly one that is closely linked to you personally, such as weight loss - try and keep it to yourself so that premature praise won't trick you into thinking you've already made it!

Person Praise Vs Process Praise

As I've just proved in my first point - praise can have a huge effect on our motivation. But, there are two different *types* of praise that could make even more of a difference.

And they're both pretty self-explanatory.

Person praise is feedback that is related to you; 'You're so clever! You have a natural talent!' etc.

Process praise is feedback related to the methods that you take; 'That's a good way to do it! What an excellent strategy!'

When you're letting people know your aims and goals, it's largely person praise that you're going to get - as process praise is something you're more likely to receive after the fact. Well, as it turns out, as wonderfully uplifting as person praise is. (I don't think anyone can deny it gives you a little bit of a buzz!) It can actually be a lot less motivating in the long run than process praise - particularly if you've already failed at something and are giving it another try.

Studies have suggested that being praised for a trait that you have little to no control over could even be *less* motivating than receiving no praise at all!

For example, let's say you've announced that you're going to start studying quantum physics, and everyone has gushed about how clever you must be.

Then you fail your first exam, and your motivation to continue is severely affected - in fact, in some cases, you might just quit altogether. However, if people had responded with process praise ('I think it's brilliant that you sit and revise that text book every evening'), you're more likely to achieve your goal - even if you fail at first.

Basically, if someone you know is a 'person praiser' - I'm thinking your mum and possibly your best mate - maybe don't tell them if you have a big goal in mind - or you could end up less motivated. Or, if you do tell them, ask them to only praise your processes...or simply don't praise you at all until the job is done!

Negative Feedback Could Just Stop You Altogether

It's really not going to come as a surprise to learn that if you share a goal or aspiration and then receive any negative feedback about it that it could put you on your arse and make you give up altogether.

And this is more likely to be true if this is your first rodeo.

Let me explain.

Imagine you've set yourself a goal for the first time in your life - a real goal with a proper plan in place of how to achieve it, and an end-date in mind. 'Beginners' are always a lot more concerned with proving their commitment to a goal than someone who's been around the block a few times.

This means that they are more likely to stick to their goal when they get positive feedback - anything negative could bring them crashing down. Whereas an 'expert' is more concerned about their progress towards their goal rather than proving that they really want it, and so are more likely to stay on schedule even after receiving negative feedback.

Want an example?

Say you want to run a marathon. You're an experienced runner, so you naturally share that goal with other runners who can most likely give you critical feedback on how you can improve and prepare yourself for said marathon. And if the world of running is new to you, and you decide that you're going to start training for a marathon, you'll naturally want to share your goal with someone who will only give positive feedback and encourage you.

And so, in a nutshell, sometimes it's better to keep your mouth shut when it comes to your goals and dreams. Positive praise is brilliant of course and feels really motivating, but it's not going to necessarily make you achieve what you want.

If you're someone that gets a high from the big 'well done' when you first make the announcement, and then eventually cools off the idea and simply stops trying altogether, next time try just quietly achieving your goal without making a big song and dance about it first.

People will eventually see the results for themselves - and then you'll have earned the praise. And, if not, at least you can try again when you're ready without feeling like a failure.

15. EXTERNAL THINGS

"External things are not the problem. It's your assessment of them. Which you can erase right now." – *Marcus Aurelius*

Wow, that's a deep one, and I think what Marcus Aurelius was saying here is that it's not about what happens to us, it's about how we deal with it that counts. Of course it's another one of those things that's easier said than done though, isn't it?

Let's be honest, we all get caught up in how things 'should' be, and it ends up causing us every negative feeling - anxiety, fear, contempt...it's not pretty at times.

Marcus is telling us to practice accepting reality, for the sake of our mental state. That's not to say of course that we should just 'roll over' when bad stuff happens, but we need to change our mindset, and our expectations. This is where the, 'which you can erase right now' part comes in: We need to learn to take control of our reactions and emotions so that we don't drive ourselves nuts when things don't turn out the way we hoped or planned.

But how?

With mind control.

Your own - not other people's.

Our mind is our greatest asset, and yet can be our biggest enemy; how many wars have been waged in yours? Probably more than you can count. It's common for people to say 'I can't help how my mind works' - but that's not actually true. You can choose how you perceive and deal with the things that do or don't happen to you.

It's not about denial and pretending it's not happening, it's about consciously choosing to see and think about things differently.

And I'm going to tell you how.

Stop Blaming External Factors For Your Unhappiness

The blame game is a very easy one to play, and some of us indulge often. You're unhappy because you're overweight, and you *would* do something about it... but the gym around the corner has closed and a new cake shop has opened right next to where you work, and that's not your fault. It's not your fault you're unhappy at work either - your boss and colleagues are to blame.

Your money worries are all down to the fact that you didn't get that promotion at the beginning of the year, your lack of social life is the fault of friends getting new jobs with different shift patterns, your relationship is going down the shitter because people keep popping up with unsolicited opinions and advice...

Now, I'm not saying those things aren't happening, or that they're not playing a part in why you feel so crappy - and I'm not saying you should ignore them. But, what I *am* saying is that, instead of bitching and moaning about it, reset your mind and choose to react differently.

See the gym closing as a good thing; a morning jog is free, and the fresh air is good for you. Turn the work and money situation into a positive by pursuing a new career and setting a monthly budget to save money. If you're stuck indoors more often than you'd like because your mates aren't around as much, increase your social circle by taking up a new hobby or interest...and if people are sticking their nose in where it's not wanted, tell them to piss off, and focus on what *you* think and feel about your relationship.

There's probably even a lesson in willpower to be learned from that cake shop opening up - I dunno.

The point is, if you spend all your time blaming other things for your unhappiness, you'll never be happy. Use external factors as a catalyst for growth and change.

I know it's cliche to say, but the only person who can make you happy is you.

If you're making someone or something else responsible for it, you're giving them too much power.

Don't Let Other People Bring You Down

I know I've spoken about this before, and I'm not talking about not being there for people who are genuinely having a hard time. Being a compassionate and empathetic person who other people feel able to turn to for comfort, advice, and to lift their spirits is a wonderful thing - well done, you.

And we all know someone who finds the negative in everything - you know who I'm talking about. The sort of person who would win a million and be disappointed that it wasn't two; someone who sees the worst in every situation and doesn't have a good word to say about anyone or anything.

As infectious as positivity and joy is, negativity can be too, and if you surround yourself with the sort of person who only sees the bad, you might find yourself following suit. Of course, things are going to happen in life that are bad - shit happens, and you do have to allow yourself to feel sad, angry or frustrated.

Once you've allowed yourself time to do that it's important to choose to take something positive from the situation. Be of the mindset that every opportunity - good or bad - is a chance to learn a new lesson and to experience personal growth.

Take Control

I've already mentioned power - and *you* have it - the power to choose how you perceive things. You are the one who is in control of your own mind, so when something happens that is less than ideal, it's up to you, and you alone, how you look at it.

Perhaps you've been turned down for a job you really wanted. It would be easy to assume that the interviewer didn't like you or didn't think you were skilled or qualified enough. You could choose to think the opposite; maybe you were *too* qualified -maybe they'll even contact you in the future for a different, better role.

Or it could be that it's made you realise that this isn't the career for you, and has given you the push to pursue a different path.

My point is, you can take something good and positive from every situation - all you have to do is react differently to it. A situation can't hurt you unless you choose to interpret what is happening as hurtful, and if you choose to not feel harmed - you haven't been.

Accepting rather than resisting sounds a little masochistic, but it's not about blindly accepting our fate, rather more about choosing to stop wasting our energy complaining about things we can't change, and instead channel that energy into a positive response.

Change from a fixed mindset, to a growth mindset - don't always assume the worst, but, if the worst *does* happen, accept and adapt. By changing yourself and your reaction you'll be able to take something positive from the situation.

One of the big reasons that people struggle with this is because they give too much power to the past and the future. If you don't get that big promotion you might start thinking about the other things you've been passed over for in the past, and feelings of failure are going to start creeping in.

If a relationship has ended badly you might start thinking forward about future relationships - what's the point of putting yourself back out there and potentially entering into another one? It'll only end the same way as the first - in heartbreak.

It's hard not to think forward or back, but it's pointless because we can only live in the now. We only have control over what's happening to us today - not necessarily the situation itself - but certainly over how we react to it.

There could be a million reasons you didn't get that promotion, but It's not likely related to the reasons you were passed over before. Getting dumped today doesn't mean you will in the future, so tarring relationships that haven't even happened yet with the same brush is just a huge waste of time, energy and emotion.

As I said earlier, give yourself some time to feel how you feel, and then reset your mind and try to look at things differently. What opportunities could arise from what's just happened? What can you learn? How can you grow from it?

Marcus Aurelius was basically telling us that we have the ability to control our thoughts, and we should use that power to assess external situations, rather than let *them* control *us*.

Have a watch of this video http://ashtag.team/Worry

16. BEGIN TO SPEAK

"I begin to speak only when I'm certain what I'll say isn't better left unsaid." - Cato

It is said that honesty is the best policy. And this is certainly true - never more so than In our relationships with other people. Relationships, whether romantic, platonic, with family members, or with our work colleagues and clients, certainly benefit from telling the truth, the whole truth, and nothing but the truth.

Or do they?

Are some things, for the sake of those relationships, better left unsaid?

I think a lot can be said for thinking before we open our mouths. What purpose will be served by saying what we're about to say? Should sparing someone's feelings come before honesty?

Surely it depends on the situation.

And the relationship...

Romantic Relationships

In a 'perfect' relationship with a romantic partner, both of our lives would be an open book. We'd know everything about each other, and would never worry about whether or not the other person was keeping anything from us.

After all, if there's no trust, there's no love.

And yet this is the real world, and even those in the healthiest relationships sometimes hide things from each other. The question is, where do we draw the line? - Even small deceptions can rock a relationship.

So, what's harmless, and what isn't?

It's safe to say that the 'big one', when it comes to romantic relationships, is infidelity. This is one instance where not saying anything in order to save the other person's feelings is somewhat of a no-no. The fallout will be devastating, but more often than not 'the truth will out', and deciding that that truth is 'better left unsaid' will surely eventually turn around and bite you in the arse when it comes out 6 months later.

A healthy, intimate relationship involves honesty and disclosure, and if you were dishonest enough to do the dirty, the least you can do is speak up before they hear it from someone else.

Having said that, there are definitely situations in romantic relationships, where leaving something unsaid for the sake of harmony and to spare your partner's feelings is for the best.

That new guy in the office, or that woman who has just joined the same gym as you, is hot! Probably one of the best-looking people you've ever seen in real life. Of course, you'd never tell them that, and you certainly wouldn't act on that opinion - so telling your partner that you've just seen human perfection personified can probably be left unsaid.

The same goes for the fact that you don't really enjoy the Sunday afternoon visits to your spouse's elderly father - it's only an hour out of your week, and it makes your partner and her family very happy, so why say anything?

That shirt your husband just bought is ghastly. You don't think it particularly suits him, and you don't like the fit. But he loves it and feels confident in it. So probably best to keep schtum.

You get the idea.

Friendships

Platonic friendships can be just as intimate as romantic ones in many ways. The idea that some things are better left unsaid is probably proportionate to the length of the friendship.

If you've been mates for 20+ years, treat each other's homes as your own, and love their parents like they're yours, there's probably a bit more wiggle room for speaking the whole truth and nothing but the truth.

This is especially true in same-sex friendships. Good friends don't want you to go out looking like shit, so it's not uncommon for girls to tell their mates that a dress isn't particularly flattering, or that their hair looks better a certain way, before they go out. And a lot of male friendships seem entirely centred around brutal honesty to the point of insults sometimes.

And, again, there will be situations where keeping your mouth shut is for the best.

New partners are often one such case. If you know something about a friend's new partner that could be damaging to their safety or health - then speaking up before they get in too deep would probably be considered the right thing to do.

And, if it's a case that they're not really your cup of tea, you don't think they're 'good enough', or you just flat-out don't like them, it's probably better left unsaid. Nine times out of ten you'll just end up looking bitter or jealous, and more likely than not - especially if your mate's really into that person - you'll end up wrecking your friendship rather than their relationship.

At the end of the day, it's not our decision who our friends date - even if you think they're a 100% gold-plated twat, so your best course of action is to keep your opinions to yourself, and then be there for your friend if it all goes tits up.

Family

A lot of people say there's nothing more important than family although that really depends on the family.

How honest you can be is all down to your own personal family dynamic, and it might be that you can speak more honestly to some family members than others.

The main difference between family relationships and romantic or platonic relationships, is that if the shit ever hits the fan with family - you're still related to them whether you like it or not. So, whilst there are probably few people in the world you can be as honest with as your family, you probably also don't want to tell them exactly what you feel about every single aspect of their lives, every time.

Similar to a platonic friendship, if you think the guy your sister's about to marry is a dick because your personalities clash, it's probably better left unsaid. However, if you have it on good authority that he is involved in something that could cause your sister harm or upset, you've got the right to voice your concerns.

Of course, the great thing about families in this situation is that you have a ready group of people with the same vested interest in the wellbeing of your sister as you do, to bounce the information and best course of action off.

When your mum's proclaiming proudly that you've never given her any trouble or cause for worry; the fact that you got off your face at your mates house party fifteen years ago, and that you cheated your way to that A in GCSE maths, can probably go unsaid. The same goes for when your dad asks you what you think of that awful casserole he's cooked, or when your nan knits you something ghastly for Christmas.

If speaking your mind only really serves to make someone you love feel bad, I think it can be left unsaid.

Business Relationships

In the business world, all you really have to go on is someone's reputation. And good reputations are built on honesty and a job well done.

Is there room in business for the idea that 'some things are better left unsaid'?

I think it depends on the nature of the business relationship.

For example, I would never recommend telling a customer or client that you think they're a demanding and obnoxious pain in the arse, or that you think your boss is a useless moron.

However, for the sake of maintaining a pleasant working environment, you might have to speak up sometimes - but often in a different way than you would if you were addressing an issue with a close friend or family member.

For example, telling that guy who works in accounts that co-workers are complaining that he has a body odour problem wouldn't be much fun, whereas a group email reminding the entire staff of the importance of personal hygiene in warmer weather, and letting them know there'll be deodorant sprays in the staff toilets for all to use, is a way of saying it, without saying it.

Regardless of the situation, or the people involved, Cato was definitely onto something when he suggested only speaking when we're certain it's not something that would be better left unsaid. It's always best to think about the consequences before we open our mouths.

How many relationships could've been saved if you hadn't spoken too soon in the heat of the moment?

How many uncomfortable situations or hurt feelings could have been avoided if we hadn't just blurted out the first thing that came into our head?

While we can all agree that nine times out of ten, honesty is the best policy, for the sake of harmonious relationships, a happy work life and, quite frankly, we don't end up looking like a total arsehole, we should always engage our brains before our mouths.

17. HOW LONG?

How long are you going to wait before you demand the best for yourself?' - Epictetus

Well, there's always tomorrow, isn't there?

Sadly, no, not always...which is why the question Epictetus asked is so poignant. We should all be demanding the best for ourselves; the best for our bodies and minds...the best from our relationships, the best from our jobs... but, like most things, it's easier to either settle, or put off demanding the best for ourselves for another day.

The whole premise of New Year's resolutions is built on this if you think about it.

It's rare to suddenly come up with what we want to achieve or change on the first of January - generally we've been thinking for a while that we want to give up smoking, eat more healthily, get more exercise, get a better job... but for some reason, we don't demand those things for ourselves NOW, we wait until the beginning of a new year before we declare it and actually get off our arses and get it.

It's cool that you've decided you want better for yourself, and better late than never, but why wait? You need to change that mindset and demand those good things for yourself right now! For one, you might not have the luxury of waiting (tomorrow is never certain!), and secondly, why do you value yourself so little that you are willing to defer this improvement to your life until a later date?

Putting stuff off - like a student who has months to complete an essay but rushes it the night before - is never fruitful. But, how can we demand the best for ourselves right now, and how can we follow it through?

It comes down to revamping your self-worth - something that's normally set in childhood.

The hope of course is that you grow up in a healthy, loving and nurturing environment, where you know your value. But, for those who have spent time in an unhealthy emotional environment it can be all too easy to not have a clue about self-worth.

And it swings both ways:

If you have little self-worth, chances are you view yourself as undeserving and not good enough. You probably spend a lot of time and energy trying to prove yourself to others, and are probably self-critical and insecure.

However....

If you have an over-inflated sense of self-worth, the opposite may be true, and you might now be a demanding person who believes the world should revolve around you, and someone who becomes emotionally immature when that doesn't happen - the adult version of a spoiled brat, if you will.

How do we achieve balance?

Change The Way You Talk To Yourself

If you want to increase your self-esteem, changing the way you to talk to yourself is step one.

You need to change the inner dialogue that's telling you you're not good enough or that you have to constantly try and prove your worth. When that little voice starts up, cut it off and flip the script. You *are* good enough. You *do* deserve good things.

You need to change that inner dialogue as well if it gets angry when people aren't bending over backwards for you.

If you're constantly expecting other people to placate your needs you're only going to end up disappointed when your expectations aren't met - it's not the job of other people to make you feel worthy.

Basically, there needs to be a balance between what you can realistically expect from others, and what you need to do for yourself.

YOU need to work on being good enough for YOU - so make sure your inner voice knows that!

Create Your Own Happiness

Happiness doesn't just happen - you have to create it yourself.

If you don't, you'll start seeking it from outside sources, which can manifest itself as neediness or pushiness. This type of behaviour can be very draining for those around you. If they constantly feel under pressure to make you happy? Eventually they'll bugger off.

You deserve good things. You deserve happiness and love. If you truly believe that, and tell yourself that - either by writing it down or repeating it to yourself in a mirror as an affirmation (I promise you that you'll only feel like a prat doing that the first few times), you'll start to attract all of those good things that you deserve.

Work Hard

We all know that hard work trumps genius, so if you're thinking that you can't demand better for yourself because you don't have a degree, that's bollocks.

You don't need an IQ that's through the roof to be successful - those that work hard are the ones who succeed at the highest level, and a wonderful byproduct of achievement and of working with purpose, is the aforementioned happiness.

There is very little in life that makes you feel as good about yourself as the sense of achievement that comes from being committed to what you do, and the success that comes from that brings with it self-respect, self-esteem and self-love.

Soon you will come to demand that success, and so you will work harder towards it, and become more successful...and then demand more...and so it goes on and on...

Invest In Healthy Relationships

Sure, we should be demanding the best for ourselves, rather than relying on other people to give it to us - but that doesn't mean we should be content with surrounding ourselves with shitty people.

Just one toxic person can completely destroy one's entire sense of self; so choose people who treat you with love and respect. Refuse to be a part of relationships where there is a hierarchy, or where you have to constantly prove your self-worth in order to keep their love or friendship.

Conversely, don't *you* be that shitty person! - don't be the one who makes too many demands of others in order to make you feel worthy. Remember, it's not someone else's job.

Rely On Yourself

We come into the world alone and we go out alone, and while healthy relationships are important and enriching, a healthy self-esteem can't come from relying too heavily on other people - it will make you lazy and entitled!

Learn to take control and support your own life; don't allow other people to do for you what you can do for yourself. Becoming a whole person, someone that you know is worthy, someone that you admire, respect and trust - and, most importantly, can rely on - is going to help you no end when it comes to demanding the best of life for yourself.

Be Happy For Other People

People with healthy self-esteem are so satisfied with their own lives, relationships and careers to be jealous of other people - and this is mostly because they like who they are and are happy.

This makes it easy to be happy for other people - there's no need to be jealous because you feel that someone else is hogging all the love or all the success, because that's not how it works. There's enough love, happiness, money and success for everyone, and once you realise this, the success and happiness of other people isn't a threat to you or how you view yourself.

Eat Healthy

Fueling your body for a positive mood and for productivity makes it easier to start demanding the best for yourself. If you're sitting around full of crap and feeling sluggish, it's hardly going to motivate you to go out there and grab the best life is it?

If you feel healthy and happy, and are supplying your body and mind with all the nutrients that they deserve, your self-esteem and self-worth will flourish.

Exercise

Hand in hand with healthy eating comes exercise. There's not much that lowers self-esteem quicker than not liking what you see in the mirror, and regularly exercising can make you feel much better about your physique.

It's not just about the aesthetic of course

Feeling strong and appreciating what your body can do can promote feelings of gratitude and positivity - not to mention that exercise is the best antianxiety and antidepressant around!

Commit to some exercise, get outside into the world and appreciate how much beauty is around us, and how much we have to be thankful for - it's great for the mind, great for your self-esteem, and a great motivator for demanding the very best for yourself.

Come on Do It Now!

18. WASTE TIME

'Waste no more time arguing what a good man should be. Be one.' - *Marcus Aurelius*

When Marcus Aurelius wrote these words almost 2000 years ago, he was basically saying that it's not what we say - but what we *do* that counts...in other words: less talk, more action is what's required, and that's just as much the case now as it was back then - maybe even more so.

Let's face it, we all love having the last word don't we? We all want our opinions to be heard, and our views to be thought of as 'right', and agreed with. That's why social media platforms are rife with discussions, debates and arguments - about government, the environment, conspiracy theories, which big businesses have paid their taxes...

People seem to love it!

But it's just words, it's not *doing*.

And we all know that actions speak louder.

In reality, strangers who read your comments on Facebook or Twitter or whatever, will either agree or disagree - maybe even tell you that they do, and why - and then forget about it and move on with their day.

What I'm trying to say is that talking or (arguing) about these things won't move you forward in any way. Only actions can do that. Marcus Aurelius' quote is a reminder that we need to take action and lead by example in order to make any real change.

Sitting on the sofa with a bucket of KFC and talking about how you plan to have a six-pack by Christmas doesn't really mean anything....lamenting the fate of our planet while driving your huge gas-guzzler to the shop that's five minutes round the corner is just lip service.

Let's face it, we could all sit around talking or thinking about what we want to do, who we want to be, or what changes we want to make to our lives. We can procrastinate and beat around the bush for years....or, we can be proactive, take the bull by the horns and actually go and bloody DO it.

Now, OBVIOUSLY the talking and planning stages of setting goals or making life changes are important, and talking about any issue that you're passionate about or is relevant to your life is cathartic and can be a learning experience - I'm not saying don't talk (and neither was Marcus!). What we are saying is - don't put-off what needs to be done.

Why?

Because procrastination is the death of creativity, and in an age where the world holds so many distractions, it's too easy to spend our time thinking and talking about what we want to achieve, all the while telling ourselves that we'll take action 'tomorrow' - a day that won't always be there.

Why It's Easier To Talk Than Take Action

Well, it's the easy option isn't it; much less effort to sit around with your mates, moaning and putting the world to rights over a few bottles of red than it is to start a fundraiser, write a letter to your MP, or join a gym.

Of course, the results aren't the same, but in our minds we can tell ourselves that we've taken the first step - we've started on the road we want to go down - when in fact you haven't moved an inch. And you know that really, which is why on the flip side of all the talking and 'best-laid plans' is the anxiety and self-loathing that comes with knowing that you've done fuck-all really - and, as it turns out, that can be bad for your health.

A link has been discovered between procrastination and hypertension and cardiovascular disease. Scientists involved in the study hypothesised that procrastinators often punish themselves over unfinished projects and over their lack of self-discipline.

And let's not forget another downside to more talk than action - running out of time. Not necessarily in the morbid, 'tomorrow isn't promised' sense - although that is important to remember...I'm actually talking about more specific deadlines and time limits.

If you've been talking and debating about whether or not to run for your parish council - there'll be a deadline to meet in order to throw your hat into the ring. If you fancy a change of career, there'll be a relatively small window of opportunity for you to apply for a position you really want. If you want to shift a stone by Christmas, it'll be much easier to achieve if you start in March rather than in November.

You get the idea.

Talk is cheap, although not always - there's no denying that communication is the key to lasting relationships both romantic and otherwise, friendships, business relationships...but even as important as the spoken word is in all of these connections we make in life, it's often the actions that are more important, and that mean more to those around us.

The reason being, largely, is that it's easy to lie when we talk, and verbal lies are easy to believe - after all, we want to believe what the people in our lives tell us. But when it comes to actions, it's virtually impossible to lie.

You either do something, or you don't.

Areas Of Your Life Where Actions Speak Louder Than Words

The business world - whatever industry you work in, you can bet your life that at some point in your working life you've encountered a 'Billy Big Bollocks' - a man or woman who has all the right spiel when it comes to business goals. Billy has plenty to say about his huge goals, and how he's going get there. But more often than not it's just a load of hot air. The words don't mean anything and nothing happens.

 Let's look at some of the most successful businesses and entrepreneurs in the world. It more than likely took them decades to get where they are....no huge proclamations about their goals, just quietly working under the radar, step-by-step to climb the next rung of the ladder, until you suddenly notice they're at the top! That's action in action!

Apologising - Obviously a verbal 'sorry' is important. It's an acknowledgement of your wrongdoing and a promise to change your behaviour in the future.

And how do people know that you *really* mean you're sorry?

By the actions you take to change the behaviour that lead to you having to apologise in the first place of course.

Teaching /Mentoring - This one applies to the workplace, parent/child, and teacher/student situations. Actions are always a more effective way to communicate your instructions than words. You can share all the tales of success you like, and explain verbally what you want the other person to do - but physically showing them is always going to be more successful.

Respect - Telling someone you respect someone is all very well and good, but showing them; by listening to their opinion even if it differs from yours, following their instruction or taking their ideas on board is a way to show them that you value them and what they say

And so there it is - actually *doing* something is always going to move you forward...just talking about it means you're static - however good the intentions are.

There's no need to keep banging on about what you should be - just go and *be*. In the end people won't remember you for what you said you would do, they'll remember what you did.

19. OFTEN FRIGHTENED

'We are more often frightened than hurt; and we suffer more in imagination than in reality.' - Seneca

Telling someone that something is 'just all in your head' is pretty abusive in the wrong situation - particularly if that person is suffering from a mental illness of some kind, and I don't believe that this quote from Roman stoic philosopher Lucius Annaeus Seneca means anything quite so flippant.

I think what he was trying to say is that as human beings we tend to imagine the worst case scenario in most situations, and we're naturally relieved when it turns out not to be as bad as we feared.

For some people, this fear can give a euphoric rush - think about people who enjoy roller coasters or scary movies! If you think about it, these are 'safe' ways to experience that worst case scenario - despite the fact the roller coaster is hurtling towards the ground, you can be safe in the knowledge that it will follow the track skywards again.....that terrifying monster in the movie will be gone once you switch the TV off or leave the cinema, but until then you can enjoy the thrill of him leaping out when you least expect it to do his worst.

These are just two examples of fear being fun, and for people who are into that it can be exhilarating.

The danger comes when we implement that 'thrill or fear seeking' mindset into our daily lives.

It's so easy to scare ourselves into inaction - or an inappropriate action - based on what we think might happen. In our imagination we fear the worst, but how often is the reality that bad?

If you really think about it, almost never.

Anticipation IS Still Important

Of course, I'm not saying never fear the worst - but only do it in order to sort out a contingency plan! Anticipating the worst likely outcomes means that you can prepare for what you'll do in that case. (Hope for the best and prepare for the worst!)

You'll notice I said *likely*, rather than the worst *possible* outcome. If we were to constantly plan for the worst *possible* outcome we'd never do anything! We probably wouldn't even bother getting out of bed - after all, what if we were to fall down the stairs and die from a head injury? That would be the worst *possible* outcome to getting up in the morning, right? It's just not that likely.

It's said that there are no limits to your imagination, but in the case of always imagining the worst we really need to learn to reign it in - or we'll drive ourselves mad imagining all the terrible things that could possibly happen every time we leave the house, get in the car, or even take that new job.

Sure, it's possible that something you weren't expecting to happen could occur, but that just means we need to be flexible and prepare for other outcomes by thinking on our feet. Anticipation is a bit of a balancing act. Not enough and we'll be surprised far too often; too much, on the other hand, and we are constantly worrying unnecessarily. Neither of these paths are good, and both will be a waste of our time, energy and emotions.

Don't Worry

There's nothing more infuriating when you're worried about something than some well-meaning person telling you, 'don't worry about it!'

Ah, if only it were that simple - just don't worry about it!

Brilliant, thanks, problem solved!

Of course, it isn't. And even if you're not someone who considers themselves a 'worrier', we all suffer from our over active imagination from time to time. I'm sure yours has run away with you and made you imagine the worst at some point - when you got on that plane? When you stood up in front of your work colleagues to do that presentation? When you had to go into hospital for a routine operation?

At the risk of sounding like one of those idiots who says, 'don't worry', it's important to keep those rising levels of worry and anxiety at bay by keeping a clear mind when you're presented with a situation that instantly sends your imagination scurrying to the worst thing that could happen. Whether that's a few deep breaths and counting to ten, or using breathing and visualisation techniques - whatever works for you!

It's not easy to stop imagining the worst once you've started - but it can be done.

Why Does My Imagination 'Go There' In The First Place?

Aside from the fact that most human beings have a natural tendency to air on the side of caution, there's normally a deeper reason why we feel the way we do, or have a certain attitude about certain things. If you're someone who would consider themselves a 'worrier', it's most likely that something has happened in the past that has set your default mindset to, 'things will continue to go badly for me'.

This could have been a one-off, traumatic experience, or a string of what you think to be 'bad luck'. The truth is that if this *is* your mindset, it ends up being a self-fulfilling prophecy. You'll stop looking for the good in anything; missing out on opportunities and benefits because all your mind is focused on is the terrible, terrible things that have happened. And why not? You expected something bad to happen, and you were right - here it is.

You can see how this is an unproductive, defeatist and quite frankly, exhausting way to live your life.

It's important to work out why it is that you feel this way so that you can at least understand how to work around it if you can't remove it completely.

Take a second to think back to the times or situations when you feel the most worried - or apprehensive enough that your imagination starts considering the worst outcome.

Is it at work? On dates? When you meet new people? When you experience something new?

One (or more!) of those experiences have led to you developing a belief that something bad is going to happen to you - and this is what is driving your imagination.

So, how can we unbelieve this belief?

Well, you have to start with *why* you believe it in the first place. Most of us have experienced something that we would consider 'bad luck', or been in situations that make us uncomfortable, worried or fearful - but we don't all start considering the worst case scenario - either in the situation at hand, or during similar situations in the future.

So, why do you?

Do you believe that you deserve it? That you're not worthy of anything good happening to you? Maybe you don't *want* to do better?

Think of specific situations where you've felt like that, and consider that there might be another explanation.

If your date didn't turn up last Saturday and your imagination has convinced you that they saw you before you saw them, and cut and run (after all, it's what you expected and what you deserve isn't it?), tell yourself the many other - and more likely - reasons that there could be.

A lost phone, an illness, getting the wrong time or restaurant, losing your number, a family emergency.....these are all much more plausible reasons for them not turning up if you really think about it.

The same goes for that presentation you gave at work that you're pretty sure fell flat. Perhaps you haven't had good feedback because your boss hasn't made time in his diary yet to discuss it with his superiors. Maybe no one asked questions because you explained yourself so succinctly there was no need....or it could be that *they* were worried about speaking up in front of everyone - or it may just be a case of you suffering from imposter syndrome (if you haven't read my article on that yet, you really should!) http://ashtag.team/Imposter

If you clear the worry from your mind and think about it logically, these are all much more likely reasons than the fact that the presentation you worked hard on was not that good!

Bad things can and do happen all the time, but that doesn't mean we should spend our time imagining the worst in every situation. There's so much more you could be doing with your time than fretting and worrying over every last detail of every little thing that you do. Live life. Anticipate that *sometimes* things might not go the way that you hoped, but don't dwell on it.

If fear is your 'thing', save it for the screen or the amusement park, and when you're done, go home.

And switch it off.

20. WHICH PORT

'If a man knows not which port he sails, no wind is favourable.' -
Seneca

Sounds pretty deep doesn't it, but what does it mean?

Ultimately this is a quote about the importance of having goals in life; of having purpose and staying focused. When we know where we're going and why we want to get there, it's easy to see obstacles in the way as part of our journey; as something to overcome in order to get to where we want to be. We recognise the opportunities that can help us, we take chances or head in a new direction if it seems like that is what it will take to help us achieve what we want.

We 'sail' with purpose.

If we're drifting aimlessly, *without* goals, any trial or tribulation we face is just seen as a burden, rather than a challenge to face head-on, with the determination to reach our end goal driving us on. Without a goal - even a small one - we're not sailing our own boat. We're just sitting back and hoping that we'll end up.... 'somewhere.'

How can we take control of that ship and steer a new course - or get back on the course we were on before we lost our way?

There's a wealth of information out there about achieving your goals; article upon article on how to stay motivated, YouTube videos about focusing on your dreams and how to deal with failure and setbacks....and that's all very well and good.....

If you know what your goals are.

To me, Seneca's quote isn't really about not knowing how to *reach* your goals; it's about not having them in the first place. It's the not knowing where you're going that means no 'wind' can get you there. In other words, if you don't know what your goals are, you'll be drifting forever.

The beauty of having a goal is that it can be as big or as small as you like. It doesn't have to be about becoming CEO or building your own business, becoming a millionaire, driving a Ferrari.....perhaps you want to go back to school and learn something new, earn a new qualification, change your career, get out of debt, have a family, lose weight...you get the idea, the possibilities are endless.

Anything that gives you focus and motivates you is a goal.

Still *really* can't think of anything you want to aim for? Here are some ideas that might get your juices flowing and kick-start your motivation!

What's Important To You?

Without giving it too much deep thought, grab a pen and piece of paper and make a list of everything that's important to you, off the top of your head. Try not to censor yourself or be embarrassed about what you write down; your list could contain, 'my children', 'my friends', 'my career', 'my home'.....but it could just as easily include, 'reality TV shows', 'getting my hair done', 'my new golf shoes' - basically *anything* that brings joy into your life is important - even if it's something that might seem trivial or inconsequential to someone else.

Next, write down *why* these things are important to you. Some will be easy, our children and friends for example - we could probably write pages and pages about why they are important to us..... others might require you to delve a little deeper into yourself. Perhaps those golf shoes are so important to you because they not only represent a sport that is a passion of yours, but because they're the first pair you bought yourself brand new. Maybe getting your hair done is such a treat because it's the only time you get to yourself as a busy parent.

Once you have your list, read through it and see if anything pops out at you. Have you mentioned anything more than once? Are there things on your list that have something in common? Are there any themes?

Running themes in your lists; learning, fun, ambition, for example, can help you to identify what's important to you in life - and THAT'S where your goal setting should begin!

Now Set Your Goals!

Goals are something you're aiming for. Something you *want*, so, big or small, your goals should be something that inspire you.

This brainstorming session you've just done will have helped you to identify what it is you want to aim for, so now all you have to do is get that goal set in stone.

How?

First of all, set yourself bite-sized goals, so that they sound achievable. 'Lose 4 stone', or 'be a millionaire by the time I'm 30' are so vague and wildly ambitious, that you're setting yourself up for failure before you've even begun. These statements can of course still be your goals, but wording them differently - 'lose some weight and get healthier'/'take control of my finances and start saving money' - take the pressure off and make it easier to get into a growth mindset and get motivated, especially if you've never done anything like this before.

And speaking of wording things differently, make sure that when you speak, think or write about your goals, you're only using positive language. 'I want to start earning better money' is a lot more inspiring than 'I don't want to be broke any more' - which already feels defeated.

Be SMART

When you set your goals, make sure they are designed to be SMART:

- Specific
- Measurable
- Attainable
- Relevant
- Time bound

Luckily it's not just a clever acronym - it's also pretty self-explanatory.

Goals that are vague aren't helpful (we're back to drifting aimlessly on the ocean again). Make it easy to get where you want to go by having a very specific idea of where you want to end up. Part of being specific is making your goals measurable; ie: amounts of money/time/weight and a date by which you want to have made/gained/lost - that way you can properly measure your success and be able to recognise when you've actually achieved something.

And, of course, your goals have to be attainable. There's nothing more demoralising than setting a goal you don't have a hope in hell of achieving. That's not to say you should set goals that are too easy, either! Achieving a goal you didn't have to work hard towards is anticlimactic at best; but at worst could make you too afraid to 'raise the bar' goal-wise, in case you fail. No one likes a deadline, but having one for your goals gives your journey a sense of urgency and helps you to achieve your goals more quickly.

Have A Plan Of Action

It's so easy to write down your goal and focus only on the end result - with absolutely no plan on how you're going to get there! A good way to see your progress is to write a plan that includes individual steps, and cross off each step as you complete it.

This is also a good way to stay motivated if your goal is very long term, or very demanding.

Just Keep Sailing

Once you know where you want to go, you just have to get there, and that's not always easy. It's going to require a healthy mindset, determination and hard work. Even with a clear destination in mind you could still experience storms on your journey, but recognising something's in the way is the first step to overcoming it.

The best part is, that now you know which port you're sailing to, you can be on the lookout for the favourable wind.

You might want to look at this great video http://ashtag.team/MAP

21. LIVING NOW

"Think of the life you have lived until now as over and, as a dead man, see what's left as a bonus and live it according to Nature. Love the hand that fate deals you and play it as your own, for what could be more fitting?" - Marcus Aurelius

Whether you believe we are a product of nature or nurture, or a combination of the two, it's painfully clear that who we become is shaped by the people and situations we experience in life. And of those people and situations, it's the negative encounters that we tend to focus on and remember most.

The problem with that, of course, is that focusing on the negative creates a mental blinder, preventing us from feeling happiness in the now - and so, learning how to let go of the past and live in the present is one of the best things we can do for our mental health.

Obviously, it's normal to think about the past - and it isn't necessarily detrimental. We can learn a lot from our past; mistakes we'll never make again, things we would do differently if the situation were to present itself again.

Using these experiences to grow as a person and to educate ourselves is one thing, the problems start when we forget that we need to keep learning from the present, and instead rely only on the past - which is futile. Sure, you can learn lessons from what's been and gone, but you can't go back and change anything; you can only live in the now.

When we live in the now we benefit in more ways than one. First of all, studies have shown that being present can reduce stress and anxiety, which can lower blood pressure and stave off heart disease and obesity, as well as improve your overall psychological well-being.

Being mindful can Improve your relationships.

Being present means that you enjoy being with other people in the now and can make a deeper connection than if you're not really 'there' because you are constantly distracted by the 'what if's' of the past.

There's also evidence that by living in the moment we can achieve greater control over our mind, body and emotions, as we're no longer at the mercy of a racing mind that isn't focused on what's happening right *now*.

So, if you're someone who is constantly reliving and wallowing in the past (without taking anything productive from it!), how can you consciously begin to stop worrying, and start to live and learn in the now?

Don't Worry, Be Happy

That sounds like a song!

Telling someone not to worry when they are worried isn't particularly helpful, so that's not really what I'm doing here. What I *am* suggesting is that you take practical steps to calm your mind, which will help you to see situations and problems much more clearly - and more realistically! (We've all done that weird thing where we imagine a whole bunch of possible scenarios in our heads - most of which could never come true).

Calming your mind, either through meditation techniques, or simply by training yourself to stop and assess a situation before you start needlessly worrying, will reduce your mind's confusion and bring you back to the present.

This is easier for some than others. It all really depends on whether you are someone who tends to focus more on solutions, or problems. Whether you're solution or problem oriented depends on factors such as your upbringing, your education, what you do for a living...even your gender.

People who find it easier to focus on problems rather than solutions definitely find it harder to stop worrying about the past and live in the now.

Find Out What's Stopping You From Living In The Moment

Living in the moment isn't easy, especially in today's busy world. One of the reasons for a racing, busy mind is an excess of sensory stimulation. When any one of our five senses are stimulated, a thought is triggered, which then leads to another, and another and so on.

It can be impossible to slow down; the ping of a text message, the sounds of traffic, the glow from the TV screen, the scents from a million restaurants and takeaway places wafting up through your window....it's no wonder we are all so easily distracted!

So, what happens if one of those sights, sounds or smells brings back a painful memory or emotion? How do people cope with that? Generally by doing whatever they can to avoid them - relying on stimulants to make them feel good, like food, alcohol or sex, or by dulling the mind with substances - in other words, anything to avoid living in the present moment.

Qualified counsellors and therapists are trained in a variety of techniques designed to help you come to terms with past traumas and to start living freely in the now. But perhaps for you, the obstacle isn't some big past event that's getting in the way of your now.

Maybe it's a wandering, unproductive mind....a procrastinating mind...a mind without focus that is simply an endless chain of thoughts.

Perhaps you are too easily distracted - it's not surprising; what with the media drawing us to the past, and advertising to the future, both competing for our attention, it's no wonder we struggle to stay grounded in the now

Practice Mindfulness

To be mindful, is to live in the moment, as I've already mentioned. When you're mindful you are fully in touch with the reality of what is happening in the present.

You're aware of your body, mind, and emotions. It is more about observing than it is about thinking; we expand our awareness, calm our minds and emotions, so that we can see clearer.

And how can we do that in a world that is constantly trying to make us think of the past or the future?

It's all about training ourselves to observe things more objectively, without our views being influenced by preconceived ideas. Earlier I mentioned meditation and it's the golden key when it comes to practicing mindfulness. Everyone can meditate; there's no special equipment necessary, and you don't even have to be an expert straightaway.

All you really have to do is sit quietly and be aware of your breathing. If you find that your mind starts to wander off, just bring it back to concentrating on your breath. Let your breathing become relaxed and natural, and notice how your lungs expand and contract with each breath in and out.

Meditation is about spending time away from the constant barrage of sensory stimulation that we face each day, and allowing our minds to focus just on the here and now. Time is no excuse, just five minutes a day can have numerous health benefits.

Not really one for sitting still? Would you find it less distracting and more relaxing to walk instead? In which case mindful walking could be an option. And no, this isn't some bollocks I've just made up! Similar to mindful breathing, mindful walking brings you into the now by focusing on each footstep as you walk.

Concentrate on your steps; the movements of your arms and legs....if your mind wanders off, bring your attention back to your walking. Because, unlike mindful breathing, mindful walking has to be done with your eyes open (I don't recommend it otherwise). It means that as well as paying attention to your body as you walk, you can also take time to pay attention to the trees, the birdsong and the sunshine.

A mindful walk really is an enjoyable way to focus the mind and enjoy the present.

Of course, in theory you can do any type of activity 'mindfully', in order to really be in the here and now. It's just a case of, whatever you're doing, doing it mindfully, and if your mind starts to wander, bring it back to the task at hand. Mindful washing up, perhaps, mindful ironing.....mindful golf... basically giving your full attention to the task you are doing NOW, totally living in the present.

As with anything, the more you practice mindfulness, the better you'll get at it - all you have to do is bring your mind back to the present task in hand when it starts to wander. Stick with this practice, and you'll learn how to truly be in the moment, and stop worrying about the past. We can't move forward if we keep looking back.

22. LIKE A PUPPET

It's time you realised that you have something in you more powerful and miraculous than the things that affect you and make you dance like a puppet." – Marcus Aurelius

Are you easily influenced? Are you someone who gives external things the power to make you act and think a certain way?

It might not be that you are necessarily weak; it could be that you just need a little reminder, as this quote from Marcus Aurelius suggests, that you have something inside of you which is stronger than outside influences - and you need to stop giving it away.

It's hard to reach your full potential if you allow someone or something to have a negative influence over how you act, think or feel. Giving someone that kind of power over your life diminishes your mental strength and, like Marcus said, 'makes you dance like a puppet'.

We've all done it - allowed outside influences to make us lose control. We've flown off the handle at things we shouldn't have. We've let certain situations cause us to do things that we regret. Perhaps we've let people take advantage of our kindness and generosity and ended up questioning who we are.

You might be sitting there now thinking of examples where this has happened to you; where you've let things affect you in negative ways and you've been left feeling powerless.

But you could have been giving away your inner strength and power more often than you've even realised. You'd be surprised at all the subtle ways you've been made to dance - and now it's time to cut those strings, change your mindset, and take your power back.

Unsure whether this applies to you?

Pretty sure you're not anyone's puppet?

Well, ask yourself....

Am I Easy To Guilt Trip?

First of all, there's nothing wrong with being known as a kind and compassionate person - someone you can call on when the chips are down. This is a wonderful trait. But has your good nature been taken advantage of?

Let's say you have a friend who is always broke a week before payday, and once a month they hit you up for a small loan.

The first time you agree, no problem; you don't want your friend to go without, and you can spare it until they get paid. But, before you know it, the next month has rolled around and they're asking again. And then again the next month.

Thanks to word-of-mouth, social media, and your own observations, you know your friend has spent their time since payday spending frivolously, and so when they ask to borrow money from you again, you're hesitant. You think that they should budget better and get their priorities in order - and you're not sure they'll be able to improve their financial situation if you're always on hand to bail them out.

So you refuse.

Then the guilt trip starts... They can't afford to pay for their daughter's after school clubs this month and she's upset...there's no food in the house....the electricity's about to be cut off.

Instead of telling them they need to be more responsible with their money so that this doesn't keep happening, you give in and lend them more money. Because you don't want them to think you're an arsehole.

The truth is, if you change the way you think, feel and act every time someone tugs on your heart strings, you are giving them some of your power. Harness that inner power and don't give in when someone tries to play on your emotions.

You can of course still help those around you, but if you're not being true to yourself because you're being made to feel guilty, you're essentially becoming their puppet.

Do I Hold Grudges?

I'm going to stick with the hypothetical friend for now.

You took your power back, pointed said friend in the direction of some budgeting apps and gently told them that you aren't able to lend them any more money now or in the foreseeable future.

And they went bloody mental.

You were labelled selfish and a bad friend, called every name under the sun - and now you're pissed off. Even months later you're angry when you think about it, and you're thinking about it A LOT.

In the words of that nauseating ice princess, 'let it go.'

Holding that grudge against your former 'friend' isn't going to affect their life one tiny bit (apart from the fact that they're probably using someone else as their personal bank account now) - but it will certainly be affecting yours.

If you're reading this and can think of grudges that you're holding, it's time to stop. By holding on to that anger you are giving someone else your power. Stop dancing! Don't waste your precious mental energy by letting them take up any space in your life.

Do I Try And Prove People Wrong?

On the surface, proving your worth sounds like a positive thing - but that's only really true if you're doing it for yourself. If you're trying to prove a point to someone else, you're just dancing to their tune.

It may be incredibly tempting to set out to prove someone wrong when they doubt you - especially if they've been very vocal about it. But all that happens is that you expend your energy - not with a desire to succeed - but with a desire to convince people that you are better than they gave you credit for.

And in all honesty, why do you give a shit?

Why waste your energy and power on proving a point to someone who, let's face it, doesn't really care anyway, and will probably have either forgotten all about it, or not even notice, when you do.

And that leads me nicely on to the next question...

Do I Let other People's Opinion Of Me Dictate My Self-Worth?

If you already identify with the last point, there's a pretty strong possibility that you're going to answer 'yes' to this one.

If you are someone who lets people's opinions of you and what you do (or don't do) affect the way you feel about yourself, you are definitely forgetting that you have something miraculous and powerful inside of you!

It's just a fact that there will be people in life that won't like you or your choices, and you have to be OK with that. Letting what someone says or feels about you affect your self-worth, or make you change the way you behave, is one of the most common ways that we give outside influences power over us.

Do I Complain About All The Things I Have To Do?

This is probably one of the most subtle ways in which we give away our power and dance like puppets, but it's definitely one of the most common.

When we feel obligated to do something that we don't want to do, and especially if we complain about it, we are effectively making ourselves completely powerless.

You don't HAVE to do anything; no one is forcing you to go to that birthday party, pay that bill, go to work... there'll undoubtedly be consequences if you *don't* do those things, but they're still choices you make.

The key here is to change your mindset and see the good in those things; that's how you take your power back.

That party is a chance to catch up with people you might not have seen for a long time, paying that bill means you won't have to worry about getting into debt, going to work means that you can afford the roof over your head....

You get the picture.

Do I Change My Goals?

Changing your goals because that's what YOU want to do is one thing, changing them because someone else has rejected you or your idea is something else.

If you give up on your dream because you get turned down for that job, passed over for that promotion, or because someone scoffs at your idea, it means you're giving someone else the power to determine what YOU are going to do with YOUR life.

Don't be someone's puppet! Just because someone else doesn't see your vision, it doesn't mean you can't succeed at whatever you want to do. Don't let outside influences make you stray from the path you have chosen - focus, stay strong, and keep going.

In conclusion, Marcus Aurelius was right; it *is* time you realised that you have something inside of you that is so much more powerful than the things that affect you. Why are you allowing outside influences to change who you are, and the way you behave? Stand your ground, speak your mind...the power is within you.

Do it now.

23. STUPID BY NECESSITY

The wise are instructed by reason, average minds by experience, the stupid by necessity and the brute by instinct." – Marcus Tullius Cicero

We make decisions every second of every day; from what underwear to put on in the morning and what to have for breakfast, to decisions with more impact, such as those to do with our businesses, our finances, or our relationships. If you're an indecisive person, it can be a bit of a pain in the arse.

What Cicero is saying here is that the decisions we make tend to be made based on how smart we are - and while I wouldn't want to necessarily call anyone a 'brute' or 'stupid' - everyone's mind works differently.

I would associate the word 'brute' perhaps more with the animal kingdom than the human world (for the most part; there's always one isn't there?) Animals make all of their decisions based on instinct; where to shelter, where to find food, when to mate….they don't make decisions based on emotion like humans tend to do - although experience and necessity are undoubtedly going to factor in the decision making process of animals somewhere in certain situations.

The human mind, of course, works somewhat differently, in that potentially all of those things may have factored into our decision making at some point - regardless of how smart we might think we are, or others perceive us to be.

Experience can prevent us from making the same mistake twice…instinct will kick in when it comes to making decisions in a survival situation….

And we've all made more than one decision out of necessity - and I highly doubt that any of us would consider ourselves stupid, brutish, or even average of mind.

The difference is, decisions made based on experience, necessity and instinct all have one thing in common; they're governed by emotion, be it fear, love, anxiety or guilt, for example.

Are we making the best decisions we can if we bring emotion into it? Was Cicero on to something?

Do we make our wisest decisions when we use *only* reason? Can it even be done?

Not really (except for the mundane stuff like deciding what to have for dinner). It's not always possible to set our emotions aside when we make a decision - but making them based purely on emotion rarely ends well.

So, is the key to making 'wise' decisions using a combination of head and heart?

What's Going On In Your Head?

When it comes to making a decision, it's your head that's in charge when it comes to logical thought; it's where you weigh up the pros and cons and use reason. Unfortunately our head can also be our own worst enemy, and when fear or doubt creeps in, all of that reason can go right out of the window.

With a strong growth mindset and a strong, loud voice of reason you can make well-thought out decisions having taken all factors into account. But of course, we're not robots...

Taking It To Heart

Your heart is closely linked to your gut when it comes to intuition. When you let your heart rule your head you're more likely to make emotion-based decisions.

If you're not careful your heart will speak louder than your head and you're more likely to make decisions that are perhaps in someone else's best interest rather than your own, or quick decisions without engaging the brain. The heart can speak loudly and drown out the voice of reason in your head.

Bastard.

So how are we supposed to get that balance right?

Indecision leads to all sorts of negative feelings; stress, confusion and anxiety being among the most common ones, so learning strategies for making decisions that factor in what you think without discounting how you *feel* is an important life skill.

You can never guarantee the outcome of any decision you make, but following these top tips, at least you know will ensure you've gone about making it as wisely as you can.

Give Yourself Time

We do have to make quick decisions sometimes, but it's hard to think clearly under pressure. If it's possible, take a deep breath and give yourself some time to sit with the problem, consider your options and weigh up the pros and cons of the situation.

Taking the time to make a decision without rushing into it means you'll likely feel more confident about the choice you have made.

Consider All The Possible Outcomes

This ties in with giving yourself time, but any decision you make is going to yield more than one result - some that you might not have considered before you took the time to think about your decision. It's not enough to just list the pros and cons of the situation, you need to consider all the possible consequences before going ahead.

Don't Stress

Easier said than done, but when faced with a tough choice, the stress could make you rush your decision without thinking it through. You might even bury your head in the sand and avoid or put off making a decision altogether.

If stress is clouding your thinking, step away from the decision making process temporarily (if you can!). Meditate, take a walk in the fresh air or do an activity that you find relaxing and calming, and then come back to it.

Talk It Through

I'm not suggesting getting someone else to make an important decision for you, but talking the issue through with a friend or family member can give you a fresh perspective - especially if they've ever faced a similar decision themselves.

Write Down How You Feel

Perhaps you're indecisive by nature; the type of person whose mind is often chaotic, or someone who always bases things on how they feel rather than how they think. This isn't necessarily *all* bad, intuition is a powerful thing and listening to your gut is important.

Before you rush into a decision made by emotion rather than reason, write down exactly how the situation is making you feel. This will help you look at the problem more objectively; you can ask yourself *why* it's making you feel that way, and will kick start you using your head not your heart.

Plan Ahead

Sometimes a lot of the stress involved in making big decisions is down to the worry of how others around you will react. Are you worried that someone in your life is going to have a bad reaction to your decision?

Shit happens.

The best way to deal with this is think ahead about how you plan on telling them what you've decided.

Be confident in the decision you've made and tell them clearly and firmly - the decision was yours to make, even if others aren't enamored with the route you've taken. If you can explain how you came to your conclusion and that you've made the decision based on reason, it will make you feel better - and maybe at least take the wind out of their sails a bit if not bring them around to your way of thinking.

Be True To Yourself

OK, so we're finally letting the heart in a little bit here. We all have goals, beliefs and values that are important to us, and it's only natural that they're going to factor in any decision that you make - either personally or professionally.

The trick here is to recognise those and let them guide your reasoning and rational thought, rather than taking over the process completely.

You'll definitely be happier with any decision you make if it doesn't go against your own personal moral code, and allowing how you feel to have a hand in the decision making process will probably make the option more obvious than using reason alone.

Calmly considering all your options, weighing up the pros and cons, and not allowing yourself to be completely ruled by your emotions is using reason to make your decisions - and is definitely the magic formula when it comes to making wise ones.

And of course we're not wise all the time. Chances are there will be situations in life where you act off emotion and make decisions based on instinct, experience or necessity. And that doesn't make you stupid, brutish - or even average.

It just makes you human.

24. LIKE A RIVER

"Time is like a river made up of the events which happen, and a violent stream; for as soon as a thing has been seen, it is carried away, and another comes in its place, and this will be carried away too." — Marcus Aurelius

Marcus Aurelius certainly had a way with words, and this rather beautiful quote is particularly poignant because it's telling us something we are only too aware of.

Time moves fast and life is short - blink and you miss it. It feels like only yesterday we were children starting school, and then seemingly seconds later leaving school and entering into the world of work for the first time....watching our friendship circle change, shrink and grow...

Meeting our first love, then maybe our second or third... How are we suddenly 30, 40, 50 years of age...and beyond?

Where does the time go?

Everything happens so fast! Our children are grown in the blink of an eye and moving out, getting married....our grandparents, once so strong and healthy, leave us before we are ready. We watch our parents grow older and more frail....time seems to just rush past us, and there's absolutely nothing we can do to stop it.

If we dwell too long on how quickly the river of life flows, it's very depressing. But nothing stays the same, life is constantly moving; and as much as we would sometimes like it to, we can't build a dam to hold it still - not even for a second.

The lesson we can take from this quote is to enjoy and live in the now.

It's become little more than a cliched meme or hipster tattoo these days, but it holds true - you only live once, and we need to live it to the fullest.

Of course it's lovely to reminisce about past events, and we can hold onto the memories of the life events that have rushed past us, but what we *can't* do is rewind time and enjoy them again.

And it's wonderful to look to the future and to wonder about all of the amazing opportunities and possibilities that might still be coming our way - but we can't get there any faster than the current of life will allow.

What we *can* do is enjoy and make the most of the part of the stream we are currently wading through.

And here's how....

Really Live In The Present Moment

We learn from our past and we look to our future, but the only thing you can possibly have any control over, and that exists outside of your head, is the now. In order to stop dwelling over the past or stressing about what hasn't happened yet, we need to root ourselves in the present moment; in where we are and what we're doing right now.

Grounding yourself in the present moment is all down to practicing mindfulness. Being mindful allows you to live in the present moment, and involves you noticing what's around you, how you feel, and why. Getting in touch with your thoughts and feelings is important when it comes to making the most of where you are in the universe today.

For some, meditation helps; taking a few minutes each day to reflect on how you think and feel about where you are is a helpful tool for bringing your mind into the present. From here you can focus on what you are grateful for and any positive changes you want to make.

Practicing gratitude is a great way to consciously live in the present. Try writing down three to five things every day that you are grateful for; it can be 'big' things like your health and your family, or 'small' things like your morning coffee or that jacket you wanted being on sale.

It might feel a bit weird the first few times you do it, but you'll be surprised at how doing this really places you in the moment and helps you to start living life to the fullest.

Show People How Much You Care

It might sound like an obvious one, but showing your love and appreciation for those around you is a huge part of living in the now.

We never know how much time we have, so telling friends and family how much they mean to us every day is so important - one of the biggest regrets people say they have when someone they love has passed, is that they didn't tell them they loved them enough, or didn't appreciate their time with them enough.

When we are children we probably tell our parents we love them all the time, and you more than likely tell your children and partner that you love them every day....but that river of life flows quickly; we get caught up in the daily rigmarole of work and the stresses of daily life.

Take the time to share how you feel about the people you love with them every day and it will help you to stay grounded in the now.

It's not just sharing how you feel with people you know that can make you feel good about where you are today; you can brighten the day of a stranger by living in the now and giving them a compliment. If you like someone's outfit, tell them....if someone has been helpful or is doing a great job, let them know....if you're romantically interested in someone, tell them how you feel.

The end result might not be what you hoped, but life is short, so grab the opportunity while you can!

Don't Listen To Haters

Not everyone will agree with the life choices that you make - whatever they may be - and letting the opinions of other people stop you from pursuing what you want in life will stop you from living in the now.

And you'll let opportunities pass you by. Success in any field doesn't just happen - you have to push through the failure, and sometimes swim against the current in order to get to where you want to be.

Live in the now and go for it! Grab what you want with both hands! Nothing in life is guaranteed, but one day you might look back and wish you hadn't listened to the opinions of other people, but been brave, lived in the now, and just done you.

Take Risks

Not stupidly dangerous ones - life is short, let's not make it shorter - but taking some risks in life can come with great rewards! It can be something as simple as accepting an invitation out instead of staying in, visiting a new country, or applying for your dream job. It's easy to stay within our comfort zone, but it's the fastest way to feel discontented with your life.

Grab the bull by the horns and live life to the fullest! Thinking of leaving a job you have no passion for and changing career path - do it! Want to make a big change and move abroad - go for it!

Sure, you might come up against some people who think you're crazy - but it's your life, it's moving fast, and if you don't do what you want now, there might not be time tomorrow. It's cliche, but it's true that you're more likely to regret the things you don't do than the things you do - so find something new, and set yourself new goals - even if they are beyond what you think could be possible.

Know What's Important To You

The only person who will be around for every moment of your life is you, so it's important that you spend your time doing what it is that *you* enjoy. Maybe it's working hard at your career or building a business, perhaps it's spending time with friends and family, or raising your children...whatever it is, knowing what is important to you, and filling your life with it is a great way to live in the now.

Doing what makes you happy is the best way to make the most of life.

Not sure what makes you happy? Find something new - start a new hobby, take up volunteer work or mentoring... Once you have discovered your calling in life and start to live in the now, loving what you're doing, you'll feel fulfilled and will start to enjoy and appreciate every second.

We've probably all felt at some point that we want to stop the world and get off; that life moves too fast, and as much as we might desperately want to keep hold of a moment in time, it slips through our fingers, only to quickly be replaced by another moment that's just as fleeting.

By being grateful for all that we have, savouring every second of time spent with those that we love, following our dreams and seizing every opportunity that comes our way, regardless of how other people might feel about it, we can truly live in the now.

We can't make time stand still, but we can make the most of every second that we are given and make the most of it. Marcus used the perfect analogy in a river - it is constantly moving, taking us along with it - and all we can do is make sure we enjoy the ride!

25. DOES NOT LEARN

"He who learns but does not think is lost! He who thinks but does not learn is in great danger." Confucius

We're all learning from the day we are born; our minds are like sponges, soaking up new information, from how to speak and how to walk, how to read and write, add and subtract..... to how to boil an egg, ride a horse, raise our children... Literally everything we know about how to be a human being in this world has to be learnt. But no one can teach you how to think.

It's an important skill - how to think for ourselves. We can have all the knowledge available to us, but without the ability to really think about what we have learnt, we are no better than parrots repeating back to others what we have been told.

When we are young, our desire to 'fit in' with our peers often results in us not really thinking for ourselves; our teenage years seem to be peak time for this. We've learnt that smoking is bad, but our mates do it, so we follow suit.

Lying to your parents about where you're going to be and going elsewhere is dangerous - but we do it anyway....drinking under age, driving a mate's car without insurance or a licence, sneaking out when you shouldn't, taking that pill you're offered on a night out...

'When will you learn?' they cry!

The truth is, you *have* learnt.

You know that you shouldn't be doing those things, it's just that you don't *think*. And this isn't exclusive to teenagers or children. As adults who 'should know better', we're still prone to not thinking at times - even when we feel like we've learnt all that we can. But how does that put us in the danger that Confucius mentions?

In some ways it's obvious; when your mind and judgement become clouded, or emotions take over, and it can be easy to forget the lessons we've learnt. We've been taught that it's dangerous to accept lifts from strangers, but we might not engage the brain when we've missed the last bus home and decide to hitchhike.

We might have learnt from our own past experiences or from the experiences of friends, that contacting an ex who didn't treat us well when we're feeling lonely and vulnerable is a bad idea, but after a few drinks, and when our heart starts to overrule our rational thought, reaching for the phone might seem like a great idea.

It's not just the obvious dangers though - the stuff that can hurt us physically and emotionally - what about the danger to our sense of self? Was Confucius right in saying that we will become lost if we don't think?

In this age of fast media and social networks, we're under so many external influences that it can be hard to even know if we are thinking for ourselves or not. To some extent we have to conform to the norms that are established by our culture and society - and that's not necessarily bad - but it can make you miserable if you do nothing but accept everything blindly without question.

For example, we sometimes feel the need to keep up with the latest trends in order to look 'cool', even though we might have learnt through trial and error that they don't really suit us or feel good. So why do we do it?

Well, for a start, marketing people are paid a fuck-ton of money to create adverts that hypnotise us into a herd mentality...then there's the influence of friends and celebrities to take into account - and while this is common for us in our teens, again, in this world where media is king, it tends to carry on into adulthood.

We all *think* that we're thinking for ourselves; no one wants to admit that they're someone who follows the crowd for an easy life, or someone who learns but does not think.

Would you even know the signs?

Well, do you:

- ☐ Buy into negative stereotypes?
- ☐ Rarely take the time to think things through; do you act before you've really thought things through?
- ☐ Get stuck in your ways and continue to do things that aren't working for you simply because it's the way you've always done it?
- ☐ Let outside influences like your peers or the media stop you from doing what you think is right for you?

If you've just read that and thought, 'god, some (or all!) of that sounds like me!', don't be too hard on yourself. Thinking for yourself isn't always as easy as it sounds - even if you're very learned!

So, here are some top tips that might help you to find yourself again.

Know Your Shit

The more you know about something, the more equipped you are to form an opinion. So, if speaking before you think is the thing that tends to put you in the 'danger' zone, (ie; causes arguments or fall outs with friends and family), my advice would be to make sure you're proper clued-up before you open your mouth.

Of course the whole point of this conversation is to explore why we shouldn't *just* learn. So remember, once you know your shit, process it and think about it before you use it to share your opinion with others.

Know Who You Are

Developing a strong sense of self makes it much harder for outside influences to get to you - particularly when it comes to marketing companies and the media telling you how you should dress, look, feel and act; what you should enjoy and how you should enjoy it.

When you know who you truly are you know what you want and you start to do what is best for you. You have your own preferences and you have cultivated your own tastes, and that makes it much easier to think clearly and for yourself.

This is often something that comes with age. It takes a long time to know who we are, to be ourselves and become self-assured. This is why it is younger people that are more vulnerable to marketing ploys, and more likely to 'pretend' to like a certain type of fashion or film or music, in order to fit in with their peers.

As I said though, the onslaught of social media and the continuing age of 'celeb' makes it harder to know who we are - whatever our age - so if you're feeling insecure because you don't look or dress a certain way: stop! Strip back the layers of outside influence that have been suffocating you, and just be who you are.

Stand Up For Yourself

Thinking for yourself can involve a lot of standing up for yourself, in the sense of not buckling under pressure or because of feelings of fear or guilt.

Often going along with the crowd and avoiding confrontation can be the easiest thing to do - everyone wants to keep the peace! But you could be doing yourself a serious disservice. Not being true to yourself can be dangerous for your mental health and emotional wellbeing. Learning something is one thing, but thinking for yourself, and having the courage to voice your opinion - even if it flies in the face of the opinion of everyone else, will stop you from getting lost in a sea of other voices.

Maybe you're quite an introverted person, someone who doesn't like to rock the boat and perhaps feels more comfortable following the crowd. What's the harm? Where is the danger?

In order to answer that we only have to look at the benefits that thinking for yourself has on your mind:

- It helps to expand your mind and boost your brain power
- You'll earn the respect of others by standing up for what you believe in
- People will admire your originality
- You'll develop self-confidence
- You'll have trust in your own abilities
- You'll become more aware of the tactics of outside influences such as marketing and the media
- People will find you more interesting
- You'll feel a greater sense of accomplishment

The personal rewards that come from thinking for yourself are endless and gratifying - wouldn't it be dangerous to your sense of self-esteem and self-worth to *not* experience some or all of those benefits?

Learning stuff is easy - certainly in comparison to thinking. Thinking for yourself requires you to be deliberately mindful, confident and courageous.

Not easy. And, the alternative?

Losing yourself.

The FlipFlopPsycho and The Philosophers Hat.

ABOUT THE AUTHOR

Over the last thirty years, Ash has built up and sold several businesses. He owns Kent's friendliest business network group, ABC Networks, a Performance Psychology business, Electrical Contractors and a Property Development company. He's a published author, STUFF for Business, Wily Old Fox Wisdom and co-authored an Amazon best seller 'The Entrepreneurs Business Club'. You might also know him as the #FlipFlopPsycho. Search that on Google.

He is a graduate of The Coaching Academy, also of the Masterclass of Corporate Coaching from The Coaching Academy. He is an NLP Practitioner, NLP Master Practitioner and NLP Master Trainer Trainer and was trained by some of the leading trainers in NLP including John Seymour, Paul McKenna and the creator of NLP Dr Richard Bandler. He is also an EFT Master Practitioner.

He has a Phd in Business and Sports Psychology and philosophy is at the heart of his learning. He's a fully qualified Cognitive Behavioural Therapist (CBT).

He specialises in mind-set reprogramming for life success, business turnaround and cash generation. He calls it elephant training!

Ash also achieved the ultimate goal for a sportsman, by playing for England 52 times and furthermore won a Silver Medal in the Indoor Cricket World Championships!! He also competed as a junior in the European Karate Championships.

You may well have heard of his famous monthly Millionaire Mindset SYSTEMS course (now online) which is approved and certificated by the Institute of Leadership and Management!

His monthly subscription group called MAD (Making A Difference) is something you should look at. http://ashtag.team/MAD

He works with footballers in the Premiership and Football league. Also professional sports men and women in a variety of other sports including cricket, swimming, athletics, golf and tennis. He'll help you go from good to great!

A lot of high net-worth individuals are really successful financially, however, some feel that they are not fulfilled and missing something important. He helps them *"Fill that Gap!"*

If you work with Ash do not expect him to tell you what you want to hear.... Expect to hear what you **NEED**. Expect **RESULTS!**

If you are fed up with an ordinary life, and would like an **extraordinary** mentor to move you towards an **extraordinary** life, then contact Ash now!!!

To coin his favourite phrase **Do It Now!**

www.ashlawrence.co.uk

https://www.linkedin.com/in/ashlawrence/

https://www.youtube.com/user/DrAshleyLawrence

Printed in Great Britain
by Amazon

71740854R00088